Love Bomb and the Pink Platoon

Ryan Gielen

Published by BROWNPENNY

ISBN 978-0-9850493-1-7

For updates on the book, AudioBook, author and film, please visit **www.lovebombbook.com**.

Please take a second to "Like" the book on Facebook!

Finally, please write a review on Amazon, or iTunes, or both. Your thoughtful reviews are paramount to the success of the book!

Thank you for reading *Love Bomb and the Pink Platoon.*

- Ryan

P.S. the book trailer will be available on YouTube and Vimeo on February 14th. Google it and share it, if you're so inclined.

Publisher's note:

The United States Department of Defense has assured us- and requested we assure you- there are sufficient safeguards in place to prevent the following from ever taking place.

Chapter 1

1999:

Newman knelt at the foot of his made bed, and prayed to a god with whom he had lost touch around the time of the divorce. The divorce had been easy, there were only a few assets and even less money. The only people who suffered were the grown children, but they had been suffering for decades, watching two glaciers gradually drift apart. By the time it was official they were numb and grown, and fine with it, really.

It had been seven years, and Newman's small house remained a frozen snapshot of the day she left. He cleaned the rooms he used- kitchen, bedroom, and bathroom- and the rest were covered in dust. He stored his bicycle in the kids' room, and some old electronics in his study. His routine was so ironclad he had worn a pathway into the linoleum floor, from the front door to the kitchen counter where he ate dinner each night while pretending to watch the local news on a small, countertop television.

He did most of his thinking in bed, while reading from a growing stack of historical accounts of American military exploits. The failures were the most intriguing- like most students of war, he was enthralled with those confounding moments in military history when his country did not win.

The historical accounts showed, in every case, the tragedy of Failure was not its blunt arrival in one massive event but its insidious creep over time, traceable in every case through the alchemic reactions that occur when small errors in early strategy met small errors in battlefield judgment again and again. Even then, at every turn, Newman noted politicians, generals, and even grunts on the ground who had opportunities to press back against the wave of errors carrying them to defeat, but for some reason or another failed to swim strongly enough against breakers. He took a little pride in thinking this study of past defeats would, if he should ever be called upon again, prevent him from making the same mistakes as those generals who came before him. He would be a respectable leader of men, he thought. He would win.

It never occurred to Newman that every man whose defeat he studied had once carried the exact same arrogance around in his back pocket, the arrogance of perfect hindsight. Thanks in part to the historian, who, with his distance from the pitch clears the fog of war with meticulous research and presents alternate paths from Failure, and thanks in part to every man's undying belief that he is unique in some way, perfect hindsight has led generations of leaders to embrace the unearned superiority of the educated, and then fail a few years later. Sure as it was true for every failure in history, it was true for General Newman Ginger: hindsight was the starch in his shirt, the stiffness in his spine, the cock in his walk. It was the untested man's hubris and Newman had it in spades, culled from the false education that only books can provide.

He was rusty and fumbled through a few opening remarks before getting to the meat of the moment and asking God for protection from whatever evil he was about to face. When he finished he felt like the quiet school boy who raises his hand for the first time- like all eyes were suddenly upon him, even though no one else had stepped foot in this house in seven years, and in his bedroom for twenty. Was it God's eyes upon him, he wondered, or just his own shame at needing God now that caused him to feel so naked so suddenly?

It was a little after five in the morning, and he was already a few minutes late. He stood and grabbed the framed photo of the girls from his dresser. He turned it over and removed the cardboard backing, pulled the photo from the glass, and noticed the layer of dust that had settled somehow between the photo and the glass over twenty-eight years. He wiped the dust away with a tissue, then folded the tissue and placed it into his pants pocket, for emergencies, he thought.

He looked at the photo- it was gorgeous in its simplicity, his two girls with mops of dirty blond hair hanging over their eyes, their clothes in the outdated style of hand-me-downs from the 70's, sitting on a stoop outside his house, squinting in the sunlight. The girls stared back at him with polite smiles and soft faces, onto which he had always projected deep, complex minds, and sincerity, and wonder, and happiness at all the hidden richness of life. It was simultaneously his hope and his conviction that they lived with an exponentially greater appetite for the vastness of this world than he had.

He placed the photo carefully into his wallet. He did not know why. The frame that had held it was sufficient- handsome and lightweight. Surely it would be here when he got back. Yet, something told him to keep it with him now, close.

Chapter 2

Burnam carefully outlined her hips, then erased and recast her waistline to accentuate the curves beneath her black panties. He paused, studied his work, and erased her waistline again. He despised women with large waistlines, and square bodies, he thought, he despised those, too. Women should be curved in all the right places, only the right places, like his mother, god rest her soul. Now, there was a woman, he thought.

Burnam brought the waistline in on his doodle and whipped his pencil off the page with a flourish. On paper the pinup stood, her right knee angled in, her right hand on her hip, a cigarette in the other, tight black curls falling from her head.

I should've been an artist, he thought. What does it pay, drawing? I bet the women are better. Just look at this one, she's stunning, he thought.

He imagined being fucked by her. He preferred to lie still while the woman rode him. Truthfully, he was usually paralyzed by fear when naked in front of a woman, and thus had no choice. Once, in Vietnam, on a lark he told the prostitute to order him around like his superiors did, and the moment blossomed into something beautiful for Burnam.

She embraced her chance to mock him and the soldiers she had watched overrun her home, and put on an inspired performance barking orders, pacing through the room, even grabbing Burnam's pistol off the floor and waving it around wildly, pretending to shoot it into the air to punctuate each command, which is how she imagined the American soldiers approached their work. Her enthusiasm for the role allowed Burnam to escape the terrifying reality of his nudity by responding exactly as he would back at the war: by simply following orders.

She ordered him to lie on his stomach. What happened next shook Burnam to his core. Straddling his bare back, the prostitute jammed Burnam's face into the pillow and, without warning, shoved one of her tiny fingers into Burnam. He screamed into the pillow. She pushed deeper, and a wave of pain shot through him and he screamed again.

But, he did not roll over. He did not throw her off and halfway across the room, as he envisioned doing. He did not, in short, resist. After all, he was a good soldier, just following orders.

Burnam panted and began to sweat, opened his eyes and tried to focus them on the headboard, to regain some sense of place and time, but the prostitute, sensing the slightest loss of control, forged ahead, again.

Suddenly the pain was gone. The surge of adrenaline and the raw eroticism of violating and being violated overtook Burnam, and the tips of his fingers and toes began to tingle. He traced the thin line of sensation as it raced from his forearms, neck and spine, down through his thighs and calves and back again.

"You love me now," she whispered, after a short silence.

Burnam dressed himself quickly, frightened that staying in the room now would somehow alert his friends to what he had just done, and could never undo. He wanted the moment to die, the witness to disappear, the reality to- through some strange shift in the cosmos which he could not comprehend or create- become simply an erotic fiction he had dreamed under a shady tree in the jungle.

He considered killing her, but it was a fleeting thought. He had killed plenty of gooks who actually deserved to die, for which he knew he was still right with God. But allowing a gook to finger you, and then killing her… How would the Big Man react to the double offenses of sodomy and murder on the same day, he wondered? Not well, probably.

Burnam never returned, and never paid for sex again during the war. His masturbation rituals, however, took on a new and daring complexity. He discovered beads and lotions, learning to insert and remove and lube and rub in almost perfect silence, for you are never alone on a military base, even when you are alone.

Burnam took chances, stupid chances. He once gagged himself at three a.m., lying in his top bunk, and masturbated vigorously in the darkened silence. Lost in the majesty of his orgasm, he forgot to remove the makeshift gag, and thus awoke with a t-shirt tied around his head, soaking all the moisture out of his mouth and throat. It was only by the grace of God that he awoke moments before his sergeant burst into the barracks, and he was able to rip the t-shirt off, and part of his tongue with it. When he tried to scream he could only cough, and so tumbled out of bed coughing blood directly onto the sergeant's shoes. The sergeant, who had previously made plain his disgust at Burnam's general shyness, which he equated to weakness, was so infuriated by the blemishing of his shoes he remanded Burnam to clean them daily. Though Burnam detested his new role as slave to the sergeant, it was a small price to pay for the moments of glorious solitude he collected each morning as he trudged across the barracks to shine the sleeping sergeant's shoes.

Emboldened by the near failure, Burnam became reckless, masturbating in bathroom stalls, behind trees, under the table in his favorite gook café while sipping jasmine tea. It was this curious abandon that led Burnam to huddle behind the jeep with a string of beads dangling from his hand one sweltering afternoon, summoning the courage to succumb to temptation.

He had never inserted anything in broad daylight, certainly never while on patrol, but there was a first time for everything, he thought, and why not today? If the U.S. Military expects me to stay sane during this quagmire, shouldn't I be allowed to indulge myself every once in a while, he thought? Won't that help me be all that I can be? In some twisted way, he reasoned, I'm doing this for my country. This one is for America, he thought. And thus, with great patriotic zeal, Private Walt Burnam unlatched his belt, dropped his pants, and inserted a string of four beads into his rectum while on patrol just south of the 17th parallel.

Exactly three minutes later Burnam held the string in front of his face, staring at the three beads that remained. He could hear his heartbeat rattle through his shirt, echoes of imagined gasps and laughter ringing his ears, his remaining months in Vietnam suddenly becoming very, very lonely. He couldn't go to the medics, they played poker with the mechanics. He couldn't go to his platoonmates, providing the appropriate context would take hours.

Burnam gingerly shuffled with the tiniest of strides back to his barracks. He clenched his cheeks, attempting to stop the bead's shifting, but each step further bludgeoned the soft tissue with the wooden, marble-sized tumor stuck inside of him.

Inside the empty barracks he fell to his knees and began to crawl to the bathroom. He fought back tears and cursed this day as the unluckiest of his life.

A curious sound interrupted his internal monologue and he stopped, suspended on one knee and one hand, listening. Was he imagining the soft whimpering echoing throughout the barracks, or was he making the noise himself, the cry ringing in his ears yet to spill out of his mouth?

Frozen, Burnam realized the whimpering was growing steadily louder. Now he was certain the noise was not coming from his own mouth, though he empathized with it deeply. The melancholy perfectly echoed his own.

He delicately placed one hand in front of the other, pulling himself forward, marking every painful note of the soft crying as he crawled closer and closer.

Inches from the large, open bathroom now, Burnam stopped. The throbbing spread to his entire hindquarters, the act of crawling on all fours working new muscles and joints that even the most rigorous military training had failed to prepare.

He peeked into the bathroom and there, bent over a sink and crying softly was the sergeant whose shoes Burnam cleaned every morning while he slept ten feet away, being fucked from behind by a very large, very black private nicknamed "Night Train" by the other blacks.

And that is how one Private Walt Burnam became Lieutenant Walt Burnam, then Sergeant Walt Burnam, then Captain Walt Burnam and finally General Walt Burnam. He followed just one short step behind the man whose secret he kept as that man climbed the United States military's career ladder. Although the marriage was not a happy one, it was functional. Burnam, due not to a sense of loyalty but to sheer lack of ambition, kept Sergeant Mehlman's secret for some 30 years, and Mehlman, due solely to self-preservation, kept the secret of Private Burnam's dereliction of patrol duty for some 30 years. They had even developed a sort of ambivalent respect for each other, two lazy rats at sea, stuck on the freighter of life, locked in a simple, functional blood pact to keep sharing the crumbs that fell from men, riding out their days watching one another's backs for swooping seagulls or swinging brooms, with no objective other than simply not dying or being thrown overboard. This is how the perfectly average Walt Burnam, from Saint Paul, Minnesota, whose only meaningful accomplishment in life was losing a wooden marble in his own asshole, came to sit at the crossroads of history.

Burnam shaded in the supple curves around the pinup's breasts and silently thanked God that Mehlman was not snoring today, for noise from one tended to draw attention to both, and attention usually meant work.

Burnam could not tolerate the thought of being assigned work today, or on any of his remaining 17 days of service in the United States military. A real assignment, and all the accountability- orders, planning, paperwork, implementation, more paperwork, oversight, processing, and finally reporting- would ensure his last 17 days of service would be exhausting, for, once you've been promoted for doing nothing, doing anything is cumbersome upon one's psyche, and at Burnam's age, lower back and knees.

General Colt Howell, a career prick who had risen through the ranks over 32 years of dedicated service to whatever mission, objective, duty or order was being airdropped from his superiors around the world, brought the meeting toward its close.

"Bung, Boretto, get the JAG's office on this right away," said Howell in the casual style of a man who never needs to pause for questions. "Now, you all have your directives…" Howell stopped, noticing the brief, bold heading at the bottom of his directives directive. An irritated frown crept into the corner of his mouth, the richest expression he was capable of making.

"Actually," he started again, "My apologies, I almost forgot. There is one more system we have yet to test…"

Mehlman snorted violently and whipped one arm into the air like a dog chasing a rabbit through his dreams. Thirty-four generals, secretaries, aids and assistants turned at once, startled by the hysterics of the now whimpering, shaking general, who had begun to chase the rabbit with great urgency. Burnam lifted his eyes slowly from his erotic sketching, and prayed silently that all eyes were not fixed upon his partner, his mentor, his secret's keeper. They were.

Howell's eyes narrowed as he imagined leaping onto the table, sprinting to Mehlman, scissor-kicking the groggy fool in the nose and stomping him to death, then stomping his friend Burnam to death. He imagined the applause, or better, the silent submission with which each subordinate would approach him from that moment forward, for fear of being stomped to death. Really, it would only take one stomping to death, and he would have the entire base under his thumb, he thought. Then he imagined the accompanying paperwork and dropped the fantasy.

Burnam slid the legal pad slowly off the mahogany desk and pulled it to his chest like a pubescent girl hoping not to be seen shuffling between classes. He stared at the desk pretending not to notice the deadly silence, as the hopeless thought raced through his mind: if I remain still, perhaps they won't see me.

Mehlman's panting petered out, the rabbit disappeared into the woods, and true, searing silence followed. Since the outburst all of four seconds had passed, but the burning glares of 34 colleagues slowed time to the point that Burnam could hear the individual disdain leak from each person's frown. Howell's frown was the loudest, and his narrowed eyes drilled tiny holes into Burnam's soul.

In his long, illustrious career General Colt Howell had massacred unarmed villagers, assisted in covering up friendly fire incidents, wrote widely circulated press releases that painted murderous retreats and failures as scalp-taking victories, and most recently provided falsified documents to better his nation's case for launching a long-desired invasion of a small, brown country rich with oil. In short, he was the perfect general: a viciously talented and equivocating loyalist whose morality was both determined and reinforced by balancing in the ever-shifting sands of his boss's current desire.

General Howell had one other gift that greased the wheels of ascension: he was born handsome. He had learned at an early age that his looks- clean and sharp, but forever nonthreatening- created a baseless trust in him, which he fostered with proper grammar, even temperament, and eyeglasses. He could order the carpet-bombing of an entire town of civilians, or shred the very document that exonerated said enemy nation of said bombing, all while smiling calmly and speaking evenly, in vanilla tones and common words. He was most definitely a sociopath in that way, but a handsome one. Strangers found themselves thinking, upon first glance, "I like that guy," though they knew nothing of him beyond the snapshot he presented them, of a polished and pious human being. He could have been a very successful politician, but he lacked that ambition. He was perfectly happy peaking as the greatest lapdog in the game: he was safe, got outdoors often, and was always fed.

At this moment, he was considering just how to feast upon the generals Mehlman and Burnam, two worthless shitstacks who, following years of ambivalence, he decided he hated now.

Howell slammed his open palm on the table, sending a shockwave directly to Mehlman's ear.

"Let God sort 'em out!" yelled Mehlman, reflexively, startled awake. He lifted his head and took inventory, and slowly lifted himself the three inches he had slouched while sleeping.

"Morning, General," quipped Howell. "Would you like to join us?"

No, Mehlman thought. But even 17 days from retirement he knew better than to intentionally poke the bear

"As I was saying, there is one system we have yet to test, but it's a huge undertaking. I wouldn't dream of giving this to anyone but my best men," said Howell, as the hint of a crypt-keeper's grin crawled into the corners of his mouth.

Mehlman rubbed his eyes, confused by Howell's tone and angered by the direct attention and eye contact.

"Do you know what the term 'Olfactory Chemical Directives' refers to, General Mehlman?"

"Not a clue, sir."

"That's fine, quite alright, General," Howell said with faux congeniality. "You'll have plenty of time to learn while you're administering their usage on our volunteer control population."

"Sir," Mehlman began to speak but his throat was still asleep, dry as a bone.

"You and Burnam will be conducting the last in our series of non-lethal weapons tests, the Olfactory Chemical Directive, or O.C.D."

A knot slowly began to tie itself in Burnam's stomach, pulling the soft lining into itself.

"Wasn't that directive scrapped, General?" Burnam asked warily, knowing that a directive, once scrapped, then brought back, was an unclear directive and unclear directives were ultimately unsuccessful directives, and unsuccessful directives meant mountains upon mountains of paperwork that would support the military's efforts around the world and at home in exactly no ways, yet must be completed regardless of their preordained uselessness, in a timely fashion, and submitted to the proper oversight bodies in triplicate, all of which must happen before Burnam- and Mehlman- could officially retire and end this charade of a partnership once and for all.

"We tried to scrap it General Burnam, we did," continued Howell, "But Secretary of Defense Cadbury himself sent it back with a rather strongly worded rebuke, quite frankly, stating in no uncertain terms that per protocol, no matter how absurd the notion, the notion must be tested." He paused, reflecting upon Cadbury's irritating decision. "Secretary Cadbury is a stickler for protocol."

Burnam suddenly realized he had left his ballpoint pen pressed to his legal pad, and the ink had soaked into and overrun one of the sexiest drawings he had ever done in these endless meetings. Isn't that perfect, he thought, wallowing in self-inflicted sarcasm.

"What is the notion to be tested?" asked Mehlman, stretching his toes and clinching his calves, trying to send blood back into the sleepiest corners of his body.

"As was detailed extensively in your original brief some months ago, General," said Howell, "the notion to be tested is that if the battlefield enemy is stimulated enough, he will not be able to concentrate on his directive, leaving him vulnerable to our offensive. So we could, theoretically, seek to distract the enemy with said aphrodisiac dispersion device, the O.C.D."

"What, if I may, sir, is an aphrodisiac dispersion device," said Mehlman, confounded by massive words he was certain could be truncated in some way.

"It's perfume, Mehlman," growled Burnam, disgust dripping from each syllable. "We spray an enemy platoon with perfume and they become so horny they lose the will to fight."

"Why don't we just bomb them?" blurted Mehlman, "We have a target, we blow it up. It's what we do."

Howell was enjoying the equal parts confusion and humiliation he was witnessing from these thorns in his ass. "It's non-lethal, General. Capture only."

"A perfume bomb?" pleaded Mehlman. "This is a joke, right?"

"No, Barry, it's no joke," said Burnam, slowly resigning to his fate. "Just a final slap in the face for the military's least distinguished gentlemen."

General Sydney "Bird Dog" Fuller, a pockmarked, smoking, brick chimney of a man, a shameless prick for whom the middle management rung of the military was a haven- from the weak, feminine, politically correct real world, filled with its apologies and hugs, and televisions, weddings and popular music, and black people, everywhere, black people nowadays- leaned forward, a cat with two sleepy, old mice cornered and shaking. "They think it's a punishment, General Howell," he said, his Arian blue eyes suddenly as black as his lungs.

"Do they, General Fuller?"

"I believe they do, General Howell," said Fuller, warming up to the thrill of bullying these soft clams. "Now, Generals, this isn't a punishment, you know that," he growled with mock compassion, a technique he had mastered when disciplining his stepchildren. He had discovered long ago that mock compassion was the jab that lowered their guards, leaving them naked and vulnerable to the next punch, the haymaker: clear, cutting sarcasm. "This is a revolutionary program, this perfume bomb!" He paused to allow the snickering to ripple through the ranks. "We thought you'd appreciate the chance to make one last contribution to your grateful nation before you retire. And, may I suggest that contribution comes in the form of Chanel Number Five? I can't get enough of that delectable aroma!"

The room broke into outright laughter. "I'm getting flustered just thinking about it!" continued Fuller. "Is it hot in here?" He pretended to look at his lap, just under the table, hinting that the mere mention of the scent had aroused him, before joining the chorus.

Sufficiently humiliated, Burnam and Mehlman stood, saluted and shuffled out of the room. The echoing laughter all but slammed the door behind them.

Chapter 3

Newman was 54 years old and wore each year on his sleeve, in his stride, and in the lines and cracks on his face. Though soft around the edges, he wore the same grizzled expression at all times that he wore out of the jungle some 30 years ago when he was dragged out of The Shit against his will. He was not a hero, he did not love the fight, and the death, and the heat, but he thought he could still be useful. And it was on those simple terms that Newman Ginger's mind organized the world. The fighting is tough because there is killing, the jungle is tough because there is heat, leaving is tough because I can still work.

As he strode across the massive tarmac an F-14 Tomcat howled along a distant runway and Newman registered its speed. Not its power, not the grace with which 26 tons of steel can cut through atmosphere, not the achievement of man to evolve from close range skull-smashing to bows and arrows to this gorgeous, gravity-destroying art form… No. He registered its speed. About 650 miles per hour, he thought. Fast.

He stopped and saluted, allowing a missile transport vehicle to pass. He continued until two superior officers passed, and he stopped and saluted.

Somewhere early on in Newman's life he had the curiosity beaten out of him. His father's brutality occasionally leapt from emotional to physical, and as a kid, Newman had been grateful for the clarity of his father's hatred on those rare days. A beating left no room for suspense. It was the climax, and when it was over he could count on being ignored for a week or two, a calming thought in the throes of a whipping.

As a result of living on quicksand for 17 years, Newman sought out the stability of a life in service, where the disdain of superiors was constant and largely superficial. Besides, he liked the running and the lifting of the gun over his head, and the camaraderie with other soldiers, all of whom seemed to have better stories and much, much more sex, which Newman was intrigued and embarrassed by as a young man.

Newman entered the JAG offices at 0800 and his mood crept downward. The stillness of the office seemed to scream at him that he was guilty, and they knew it, and they were going to punish him. In truth the office was still because it was always still, the JAG's and their aides often working quietly in scattershot offices around the second floor, this first floor being utilized for small meetings, cleaner bathrooms, the vending machines that dispersed sandwiches- actual sandwiches, for only $1.75, in a vending machine- and storage. Newman registered the sandwiches and continued to room 110, just past the final vending machine, the sodas. He wondered how many of the 64 employees working in this building utilized the soda machine on any given day. Probably only a handful, he thought. But it's always been there, so it probably always will be.

Newman sat alone in the center of the room while six JAG's and legal aides glared at him from behind a folding table. Even the stenographer, off in the corner, seemed angry at him.

In the center of this thick wall of disapproval sat General Sydney "Bird Dog" Fuller, still high from the act of humiliating those two clowns in the morning directives meeting.

"General Ginger, I have a handball game at zero-nine-hundred," began Fuller, "so let's dispense with any niceties and get on with it."

Newman felt his face flush. He was not brilliant, he was not sarcastic, and he was not mean, but he was hard. It took a lot to break Newman, and he had decided this morning over coffee, two eggs and whole wheat toast that old Bird Dog was not going to break him today, not over this. Not over some piece of shit kid who couldn't tell his elbow from his asshole with a map and three weeks head start.

"I didn't have any niceties planned, Sydney," Newman countered quietly.

One of the faceless JAG's bolted out of his chair. "Hey now!"

The second JAG screamed over the first. "You watch your mouth when speaking to a superior officer, Ginger!"

Fuller silenced them both with a wave. "The young soldier you slapped," he lamented, "his father is unwavering in his conviction that your treatment of his son was unduly harsh, resulting in a sort of 'emotional coma,' to quote his father directly."

"And, who is his father?" asked Newman sharply.

"Chairman and CEO of our largest defense contractor."

Newman felt his heart collapse. He had humiliated a very important fuckup. "What's the upshot, Sydney? Relieved of my command? Unpaid leave?"

"You should be so lucky!" belted one of the JAG's.

"The boy had to retire to the private sector!" belted the other.

Newman saw the veins pop on the JAG's neck as he fought the urge to leap across the table at Newman, like some pit bull straining against his leash, most happy to be perfectly furious over whatever his master told him was an outrage on any given day.

"Frankly, Newman, on the table right now is dishonorable discharge," continued Fuller, opting to play the laconic Good Cop.

"Is that Daddy's recommendation or did you come up with that all by yourself?"

"You struck the son of a very important man!" someone yelled. For all Newman knew it was the stenographer. The faces in the room had melted into one giant, screaming mouth, so powerful that every word it spoke echoed through the entire universe, blocking out every thought, every ray of light, until Newman's brain exploded against the walls of his skull.

"He was a sissy! A coward!" barked Newman. "He was an affront to every man that ever fought on a front line-"

"And your actions would be a lot more understandable," screamed Fuller, "if you yourself were on the front lines, General! But never, in all my years of service has this happened in an office of the corps of engineers in San Bernardino!"

Newman slouched. This boy… This boy had screamed at him through tears, and this was before the slap. After having his third proposal rejected in as many months, the young man felt useless and unloved, and threw a hysterical tantrum at Newman in front of the entire department. The old man slapped him more for his own good than as some sort of punishment, and in all fairness, it worked. But rules are rules, and in the army, the spirit and letter of the law are one and the same, not to be parsed, so Newman would hang.

Slowly the faces returned, and they were angrier than he remembered. "Old habits die hard," was all he could muster.

"So do old generals," started Fuller. "You've been a fine soldier, Newman. Three tours in Vietnam. Two years active stateside. The last twenty four years here, in the corps of engineers." Fuller shook his head for effect. "There should be a place for you in this army, out of respect, if nothing else. But let's face it, Newman. We aren't the men we used to be. Even if you had some use to the U.S. Military, how long would you last?"

Newman felt the faces melt away again. Perhaps it was his age, but he had grown to care very little about new faces, new people, new challenges, new relationships. Twenty years ago he would've committed each face and all the idiosyncrasies of the individual participants to memory, and tailored himself to each quirk. But he was on the down slope, wading toward the end, the bottom, and new faces held no promise or hope of rebirth, so what was the point, really.

"The grim reaper is chasing us, Newman," continued Fuller. "Well, he's always chasing us, but now he's gaining ground, you see? And we're running. Running to the gymnasium, to the doctor's office, to whatever fount of youth was most recently promised. Hoping to escape, hoping to discover before we die that it wasn't all for nothing." Fuller became wistful at this last word, nothing. It anchored on his lips and in his eyes, and stretched itself to Newman across the room, an iron bridge between two crumbling shores.

"Unfortunately, so many of the things that drive us in this life also restrain us," he continued. "I can't put a 55 year-old man on the front lines of today's conflicts. I'd get my boys killed." Fuller leaned forward suddenly, the thought of life and death consequences, of maneuvers and mistakes, of battle, sent a surge of adrenaline through his taut gray muscles. Somewhere in his lizard brain the finality of death and the fleeting nature of life pulled him to Newman and Newman to him, and both of them out of this room and onto the pitch. He spoke excitedly, his face flushed, his words clipped.

"The bullets today, they can pierce ten feet of reinforced concrete. The missiles are guided by computers in outer space, these things called Global Positioning Systems, and the men," croaked Fuller, "The boys on the front lines today move silently, with surgical precision, covered in seventy pounds of body armor through the night, into the desert and back again."

He collapsed backward into his chair, exhausted following the orgasm of precision violence he had just recalled for his old friend. "They're machines, Newman... killing machines."

Fuller dropped his chin, and brought his eyes to Newman's. "Do you hear what I'm saying, General Ginger?"

Newman heard the message, but worse, he felt the message. While Fuller listed the advances in American warfare, each idea spoken and even those hundreds that remained unspoken had sliced into Newman's weathered heart and withered flesh until he was deeply cut. Without lifting a finger Fuller had successfully destroyed Newman by destroying the one thing that keeps any 55 year-old soldier alive and fighting: his hope. Hope that someday the call will come. Hope that someday he will be needed again. Hope that he is somehow, someway still useful. In ten minutes Newman felt he had aged ten years.

"There must be something, Sydney," pleaded Newman with a whisper.

Fuller began to shake his head, convinced Newman was either too stubborn or too stupid to understand that this was the end. He hated stubborn almost as much as he hated stupid, but stupid took the prize. Why was he always surrounded by *stupid*, he wondered? Did the job attract stupid, or was it drilled into otherwise intelligent people over years of service? Or was he just so god-blessed intelligent that others seemed stupid in comparison? The latter was most likely, he had decided some time ago, and that answer came back to him just this very morning in the moments following his directives meeting with those two barnacles... Fuller saw the answer unfold in his mind, the pieces of this tiny puzzle suddenly snapping together. He fought back a smile, masking pity with compassion.

"There is one thing I can think of, for the old, and the..."

"Obsolete?" offered Newman.

"Yes," replied Fuller, unaware that the compassion in his words had dissipated somewhere on the short journey from brain to mouth.

"What, then?" whispered Newman, resigned to any fate other than Nothing.

"General, have you considered giving yourself to science?"

Chapter 4

Newman moved swiftly through the hallway, over the grey industrial carpeting, toward the muddled voice spilling from the only meeting room on the floor. He passed door after door, closed, unlabeled, white.

As he approached the open door he could make out a woman's voice. Her hollow tone told Newman her voice was coming from a television, and she spoke in the clipped, clear affectation of a video presenter. Whoever she was, she sounded sturdy, he thought.

He stepped into the room and saw a thick, amiable redhead on the television at the front of the room, speaking directly to each of the men in the room. Newman caught his reflection in the two-way mirrors that wrapped around the room before sitting at the very end of the back row. He scanned the room and was disturbed by what he saw: a collection of washouts too fat, too thin, too tall, too short, too ugly or too sloppy to be talented soldiers. He fought the urge to scream at them, to scream at anyone, to find the manager or the commanding officer, to bang on the mirrors and demand an explanation. He was here to lend himself to a cause, he wanted to be surrounded by men, by real men, who were here to lend their talents to a pursuit greater than themselves, but the men in this room were degenerates, they looked as if they had been caught escaping the brig and dragged here instead of back to their cells, he thought.

"As part of our settlement with the U.S. Attorney's office," purred the hypnotic voice form the television, "the State Department has committed over the last ten years to test our newest initiatives on volunteers, instead of unsuspecting migrant workers and mental health patients."

Newman swallowed hard. So this is the final send-off in return for a lifetime of service, he thought. No gold watch, no cake, no thank you, just the opportunity to act as a pincushion for whatever horrific fantasy the military scientists have cooked up this year.

He heard the stories- M.K. Ultra, the psychotropic tests in the 1950's that led to suicides and other poor decisions, the audible torture tests of the 1970's where men were subjected to hours of looped shrieks and screams while strobe lights exploded around them, and of course, The Philadelphia Experiment.

Denial did not come easily to Newman and he allowed it to dissipate quickly along with any spare hope that he was here for any reason other than the fact that he was a warm body in a military uniform.

"Thank you for volunteering," offered the sturdy redhead. The voice seemed a little cooler now, but Newman was grateful for the courtesy, however wrote.

Over the next six hours Newman stood in several lines, queuing up to run on a treadmill, to be poked and prodded, weighed and measured, and finally to sign a stack of documents relieving the military of any duty to return him to society at any point, ever.

As he scanned the documents for signature lines he couldn't help but notice words like "in perpetuity," and "waives all rights," and "not responsible." It was the "not responsible" that stuck, playing over and over again in his mind, the record skipping on a crook in the groove.

Here he was, signing over his right to make any assertive decision about his immediate future- his meals, his transportation, his lodging, even his minute-to-minute activities would be strictly controlled by the military- yet they were not responsible for him? They would direct and control his every move and monitor his every reaction, he was certainly no longer responsible for himself, but somehow neither were they. He could not be responsible for himself, and the military refused to be, and with each signature he felt one step closer to purgatory, suspended between this world and the next, floating between his past life and... something.

For the first time since he walked out of the jungle thirty years ago General Newman Ginger felt frightened. His mind raced with the possibilities. Torture. Maiming. Chemical poisoning. Legally, with this final signature, the United States military could do anything, he thought. They could fill him with stuffing and bake him like a turkey, he thought. They could force him to eat purple mushrooms and wrestle a bear, he thought. They could get bored and just shoot him, he thought, what if they just shoot me? What if that's the entire experiment, they just shoot me and watch me die and then write a report about it, he thought? But he signed. And with his final signature he relieved them of any responsibility for the consequences of their experiment. How can you sign a paper that grants someone the right to shoot you at will, with no consequences? It was insane. He felt insane.

He saw himself scrawling the words General… Newman… Ginger… and he wanted to rip the pen from his own hand but he signed, controlled by some force beyond the hand, beyond the brain, beyond the panic. Somewhere in the deepest, atrophied, dying core of Newman Ginger there was a man who craved the freedom and the terror of a complete loss of control.

Chapter 5

Newman shuffled toward the camouflaged school bus and for the first time in his life hated camouflage. Why do we have to camouflage everything, he thought? This obsession with camouflaging- camouflage water bottles, camouflage notebooks, camouflage underwear- was so typical Army. "Do it this way because we've always done it this way," he scoffed. Newman bitched loudest in his own mind, and even then it was barely more than a fleeting whisper, but after this morning's humiliations, the voice in his head was screaming. It's a goddamn school bus, he thought. You want to camouflage a school bus, paint it yellow for Christ's sake. The surest god damn way to reveal that you're transporting our boys up and down the highway is by putting them in the only vehicle painted with what appear to be giant swaths of green and brown puke, Newman thought.

The sight of the gaggle he would be boarding with interrupted his internal outburst. If the men in that presentation room this morning were degenerates, Newman thought, these were their offspring: more slovenly, more gawky, more… pathetic in the special way that only someone born of two pathetic degenerates could be, for with degenerates, Newman imagined, the offspring wouldn't borrow whatever complimentary traits they could scrounge together from each parent, but instead would be left with the worst of each, rather like the effect of multiplying decimals over and over again, with each iteration exponentially more degenerate than the degenerate iterations that proceeded it, the special curse of degenerates being that they couldn't even get reproduction right.

JABOA, he thought to himself. "Jah-boa" was an immediate dismissal of that which one does not care for, a group who cannot hold their own, a joke. If there was one thing the military did well it was acronyms, and JABOA was a real peach, a pristine, perfect phrase whose finality was devastating and total. JABOA. Just A Bunch of Assholes.

Dismissed. Worthless. Over. JABOA.

The men stared back at Newman blankly as he approached. He could sense their weakness in some hidden, visceral sixth sense that all animals have, the ability to feel the shape and texture of another's fear. Their weakness angered him, because it reflected the fear in his own belly, an aggressive and climbing fear that he tried to bury and deny every moment of his life. It had no name or face, he had never bothered to identify it because identifying the fear would require acknowledging the fear, and the only guttural instinct Newman had that was greater than his fear was his desire to prove himself fearless. That was strength, that was masculinity, that was survival in a man's world. As a result, the harder fear tugged at its chains in the recesses of his gut, the faster Newman had to drench it, to bog it down with the only thing powerful enough to sedate it for an evening's peace: booze. He was never an angry drunk, or a violent one, just a quiet one. He drank out of a highball glass, never from the bottle. He drank at lunch and at home, never at work. And he drank until this terrifying world didn't exist anymore. He claimed, to himself, the booze brought him closer to whatever historical battle he was reading about, and each night the liquor placed him on the pitch because he washed out every other setting. And each morning it would all come spilling back, the mud of reality filling in the valley left by the flood of whiskey the night before. By the time he pissed out the whiskey each morning, the vastness of the world- the cars, the politics, the speed- had spilled back into his consciousness and awoken the fear, which immediately tugged against its chains. Though Newman refused to acknowledge the fear, he certainly felt the tugging, which he had come to know only as that knot in his stomach. That knot in his stomach. These last 24 hours he felt the knot move. It was growing, he thought. The army doctors had told him to quit drinking, and he had tried once, and the knot grew, and he drank again. This knot was something else, he thought. A tumor they hadn't seen, perhaps. Now it was growing and gathering strength as Newman became weaker, soaking in others' weakness, feeding off of others' cowardice.

Newman scowled when the men didn't stand. He outranked every one of them, and unless they were blind as well as dumb, they should've seen the star on his lapel. This particular batch must've been hidden in a closet somewhere so as to not dispirit the degenerates, he thought. One boy stood, leaped to his feet actually, and saluted.

Newman saluted in return, and handed his bag to the kid. Newman studied the boy and noted he must've been 19, still covered in zits, with patches of smooth skin where hair and stubble should have been. The boy barely filled his uniform.

The school bus doors flew open and the driver pulled a clipboard from the dash, and stepped out to call the men. "Name and rank as you board."

"General Newman Ginger," barked Newman as he brushed past the driver and stepped onto the bus.

The boy followed. He was so excited he dropped Newman's duffel when he saluted the bus driver. "Sir, Private First Class, James Aaron Richards, sir!" He leaped onto the bus and forgot all about the general's bag, and his own.

Dwight Butterman was next to step forward. In his duffel were comic books, candy and several pair of socks and underwear. Due to his aversion to exercise, he sweated profusely and randomly. His heart would attempt to force movement upon him by beating rapidly for a few minutes of almost every hour, and though Butterman was able to quell his legs' mutinous attempts to run, he was never able to fully quiet his beating heart or dry the damp crevices of his layered skin. As a result he was always uncomfortable, always seeking a seat near an air conditioner, or a window in winter, and always changing his sweat-soaked socks and underwear. He didn't like walking, or standing, because he believed both motion and effort made him sweat, so he did both as little as possible, which occasionally led to bedsores that caused great discomfort. The discomfort of course caused him to shift in his seat for relief, and that motion caused him to sweat, and he was forever generally flummoxed by the undefeatable circular nature of discomfort, motion and sweat. The harder he tried not to move, the more he sweat, and the more he sweat the closer he came to jumping off a bridge or some high building, or possibly moving to Canada, where he could be seated and cold all the time. "Dwight Butterman," he said, almost like a question. "Private, First Class." He took one step at a time, and used the intervening seconds to scout for an open window.

Terry Stryker was next. He was a sinewy, short, rat of a man who never wanted to be in the Army, but never bothered to look for anything else. So, upon graduation from his state university in the deep, deep South, he enlisted. Not out of conviction, but out of a lack of imagination. Somewhere around the age of 14, Terry had turned off, and no-body and no-thing had ever turned him back on. He spent the next seven years slouching, with arms crossed, scowling through a series of barista and temp and food service jobs. And today, as he stood in front of the bus driver without a duffel, without so much as a change of clothes, he crossed his arms, scowled, and waited for the bus driver to ask him for name and rank.

The bus driver stared at Terry Stryker, and waited. "You deaf?"

"Terry Stryker, I'm a private, first class." Terry practically spat the words, and closed the laconic scene with a half-assed salute that looked more like someone swatting away a fly than acknowledging a superior.

The bus driver snapped. "I'm uh?" he barked. "I'm uh? You think I need you to tell me you're talking about you? You think I was under the impression that perhaps you were introducing the gentleman behind you, like some kind of nightclub act? When you speak, son, you speak about yourself, and you say it like it matters." The bus driver reminded himself that this particular group was a lost cause. The investment would yield no return. "Get on the god damn bus and let the scientists sort you out."

Terry Stryker willed himself onto the bus and Andrew "Andy" Lincoln strode forward and tripped over a small rock. It wasn't so much the rock, but more his concern over what exactly he had kicked, that caused him to look down and lift his foot at the same time, suspended in mid-step while his body's inertia carried him forward. The sudden movement caused his black-rimmed glasses to slip off his face and he tried to pin them against his body without setting his foot down before knowing what exactly he had kicked- it could be a rock, but it could be a turtle or a frog, or a child, another living creature, he thought. He caught the black-rimmed glasses just before slamming chest-first into the ground. The glasses shattered into a half dozen pieces, but the rock remained in tact and left a throbbing bruise to remind him of what happens to people with the best intentions. He was legally blind without his glasses, and barely better with them.

A forgettable dope, he was average height, average build, and so eager to be liked that people deeply disliked him. He tended to watch more than speak, and to groups of men this was greatly disconcerting, and he would typically not be allowed to socialize in said groups, or they would disband upon his arrival. On the few occasions he was included, he would repeat whatever opinion was most recently stated or most passionately supported, and then- and this drove even the most patient and altruistic to abandon him- he would stare directly into someone's eyes and wait for their agreement. His desperation crawled up men's spines and ripped at the soft flesh at the back of their necks until they couldn't look at him anymore. "Private First Class, Andrew Lincoln, sir!" he yelled, excited by these new faces. Even the bus driver had to look away.

Lamar James stepped forward, a black man of no consequence, authority or significance, at least in his own mind. Though he had many friends, most of them women, or other shy, intelligent men, Lamar never associated his pristine reputation with social capital. He believed his quiet voice and interest in books made him weak, as did his desire to enjoy solitude, calm and tea. In the moments he felt strong, he would invariably turn on the television, go to a movie, or open a magazine and be reminded that real black men were militant, loud and proud, whether they were gangbangers or pundits, comedians or preachers. He grew up in a suburb of Brooklyn, his father was a lawyer and his mother was a high school principal, and they were married for thirty years this year, and he never felt so small as when he watched television, searching for even one representation of himself or the parents he worshipped. In fact, the only occasions where he saw himself represented in the world were in newspapers, but newspapers were flat and dying, and there were rarely pictures, and Lamar knew that when the newspapers die, so will the average black man. When the newspapers die, he thought, so will nuance. We'll be left with cartoons of our "community", represented to the unthinking masses as biography, and eventually we'll become the cartoons and prove every cynic, white and black, right. He never knew who to blame, and he didn't give it much thought because if he pinned down someone to blame he would probably be compelled to write them a letter or some such futility. Instead he wrote to himself, in a series of journals, his pockets stuffed with notepads big and small. The notebooks were, in fact, all he brought on this journey. "Private First Class, Lamar James, sir." He saluted and moved on.

Alberto "Chico" Cruz stepped forward. He smiled as the bus driver studied him. Chico was born out west, first generation, and joined the army for the money. He had particularly liked the Mexican-American recruiter he met during his junior year of high school. The recruiter was cool, handsome, and shared many stories of fucking beautiful women with huge tits while overseas. Alberto, a virgin, signed up for service on his 18th birthday. He liked guns and video games, and hoped to shoot people eventually. He didn't particularly wish to be sent to war, but he wouldn't mind. He believed in God. "Private First Class, Alberto Cruz!" he called, and boarded the bus. He was 19.

*

Butterman tried reading a comic book but the camouflage school bus had no shocks to speak of, and every crevice in the road felt like a crater, and even though at first the bumpy ride added a dimension of liveliness to the flat, colored panels he was reading, after twenty minutes it became nauseating and he was forced to abandon the comic book in favor of pouting and sweating. Richards stared out the window at the passing redwoods, soaking in the milky dew scent from the forest in an attempt to overcome the diesel fumes that filled the interior of the bus. Private James tried to sleep, but couldn't. The thunderclap of each pothole exploded first against his body and then against his brain and he spent the trip wondering how, if we can put a man on the moon, we can't also put shocks on a school bus. He wondered what the constantly arrhythmic, explosive sounds must do to the psyche of a child riding to school at 0700, bouncing around without seat belts, ricocheting off the steel, padless walls of this tin can with wheels. He felt angry on their behalf, and on behalf of the teachers who must then wrangle the stressed, confused psyche's and refocus them, and angry about the wasted energy usurped by this disaster of design that was both mentally devastating and cost effective, and angry that its cost-effectiveness would keep it around for decades still.

Motherfucker was the only thought floating through General Newman Ginger's mind. The diesel fumes and the potholes and the roaring of the thirty year old engine and the empty seats all around him- the bus could hold 60 men and here were seven- were so overstimulating that the only thought his tired mind could muster was Motherfucker. He was, in a word, hopeless.

Any notion of contributing to an important experiment was lost when he saw the men he was surrounded with. Would they send this bunch of used candy wrappers to a lab for something relevant, he thought? Of course not. You send this group for target practice, he thought. These punching bags, he scowled. Any hope of collaboration, or intellectual contribution was lost in the first ten minutes of the bus ride, when a few of these walking, talking turds attempted conversation: someone said something about the weather and someone else said something about tits, and then the bus hit the highway and nobody could hear anything while sitting so far apart and instead of moving- and this was probably the one intelligent thing these men were going to do the entire trip, and it was out of sheer laziness- they all remained in their original seats, and just kind of bobbed their heads for a few seconds before facing forward and settling in for the bumpy ride to who-knows-where. Further, any hope of bonding as a unit and banding together in the face of whatever adversity was shot at them was lost because of the size of the group. Seven men alone- seven!- could never win a battle, let alone a war. Seven men are not a unit, they're a fracture, a mistake, a body count.

These thoughts coalesced in Newman's mind into one word, Motherfucker, and he repeated it to himself for the entire 22-hour ride. Every exploding pothole, every glance at the other men, every moment: motherfucker, motherfucker, motherfucker. He was only a touch relieved that, for some reason, the onslaught of random pothole explosions and the unknown destination and the mysterious nature of the experiment was not bringing him back to The Shit, to Vietnam. The randomness of the gunfire, the invisible assassins tucked into the jungle, Vietnam had waged a mental war against Newman and his platoon, and they had won, and those who survived could not handle noise, or stress, or the unknown. The army had a word for it, they had gone to the trouble to at least label this phenomenon, but that had taken decades, perhaps because of paperwork, perhaps because once a soldier leaves the battlefield his usefulness to the army is debatable and therefore so is their attention to him. Newman had learned this firsthand when he attempted to receive some psychological care for the night sweats, the terror dreams, and the domestic discord they were causing.

It took him years to admit any of it, and then years to muster the strength to be weak, and when he finally sat across from the head shrink he was given a bunch of pills and a couple pamphlets and sent on his way. He never took the pills, never read the pamphlets, and years later his marriage ended and now his career, and he bounced along Highway 5 North not really thinking about any of this, but only, Motherfucker.

They drove into the night, and Newman convinced himself the potholes were fewer and farther between. He gratefully couldn't see the other men unless a car passed on the highway and its lights revealed the six bouncing silhouettes.

He looked out the window and saw a sign, "Welcome to Washington," which startled him because he didn't recall leaving California or entering Oregon. But here they were, and in the distance the snowcapped top of Mount Saint Helens troubled him. It was as if he had put on the wrong glasses this morning and each passing wonder could only be seen through the prism of the coming torture. With the unknown lurking and these lumpy scoops of table scraps surrounding him all he could see was death.

He began to feel the creep of exhaustion, the thickness of his own neck and shoulders pulling him into the seat. After 22 hours on high alert his body began to soak in the new night and initiate Newman's evening shutdown. First the limbs went limp, the muscles and joints haphazardly unclenching for the first time all day. Second the mouth- losing the signal from Newman's brain to grind teeth and purse lips- flopped open, collapsed against the soft sand of Newman's chin and chest. Third and finally, Newman reached for his flask. His hand dug under the seat and felt nothing. He wiggled it left and right, sure he would brush against the rough canvas of his duffel. Nothing. Motherfucker, he thought. He looked around the bus for Private Richards, but at this hour he couldn't tell anyone from anyone, so he did the only sensible thing, he shouted.

"Richards!" barked Newman. "Richards!" Heads lifted, eyes blinked. Newman still couldn't tell who was who, even now that they were starting to wake. "Richards!" he continued. Yawns could be seen in silhouette as arms stretched upward. He felt his dry tongue and smacked it against the roof of his mouth. Newman wanted a sip and he wanted it now.

"Rich-" began Newman, but the bus swerved right and the platoon gasped and chirped. Suddenly the potholes were constant, exploding all around them. Tree branches scraped against the windows. It felt as if the bus were tunneling into the earth. Dust and dirt encircled the bus and suddenly more branches, constant branches smacked the bus from every direction. Newman felt himself tossed into the air, each exploding pothole sent him up and down and back up, and he grabbed onto the seat back in front of him with one hand and ripped his bouncing glasses off his face with the other, and this is exactly what it must be like to die in a plane crash, he thought. The noise surpassed the concept of volume and crossed into experience, and all Newman could do was wait for it to end, which he knew in his churning gut was going to be with a sudden and stunning crash, likely into the side of Mount Saint Helens. The bus hit an exceptional divot and the explosion jammed Newman's spine onto itself and he was certain he had been ripped in two.

The platoon gasped as the bus broke into a clearing and skidded to a stop. Silence. Newman could hear the confused, half-formed words begin to spill out of the other men. The bus driver muttered some words into a walkie and Newman felt safe again. This was part of a plan. A shitty, lumbar-destroying plan, he thought, but a plan nonetheless. Newman felt safe around plans. A good outline was like a warm blanket, an itinerary was hot soup on a cold day. The simple act of scribbling down in rational order all the necessary steps of an activity assured him the activity would get done, as if knowing the process equated precisely to completing the process. In the Army it often did and in Newman's life, it always did. There was safety in a plan, you could give yourself over to a plan, and he did, he always did. Tonight was no exception. Thank god, he thought. Someone has a plan. Someone is in charge.

Butterman sniffled. Newman looked back and saw the lumpy private wipe his nose with the back of his hand. Dear god, thought Newman. I need to watch that one. When the shit flies, he'll be the first to duck.

The bus driver stood. "Company!" he shouted. "Move out!"

The men groaned and creaked, and pulled themselves out of their seats, legs still shaking from the turbulent landing. If Army men were typically machines, these were old gas stoves. They needed to be kicked to life. The pilot light needed to be jarred, its loose connections shaken into place for even a single flame to spark.

Newman resolved to find his bag later. Time to be a leader, he thought. He stood and stomped swiftly off the bus. One by one the men followed, stretching and yawning as he led them to a small pool of light a few feet from the bus. They mumbled to themselves, and slogged their way over, as undisciplined about movement as they were about hygiene.

The bus driver stepped out and counted the men. When he reached seven he turned, climbed back onto the bus, and tugged the steel handle to shut the doors.

Newman froze. I still need the plan, he thought. Certainly this man would not leave without at least handing me a piece of paper, or a dossier, surely we wouldn't be abandoned, he thought, as the bus growled to life and reversed into the forest.

Chapter 6

Burnam stretched his arms toward the ceiling. He was always wary of doing so because occasionally his shirt would untuck just as a subordinate would enter the room, and he would have no choice but to unbuckle his pants, unzip his fly, and carefully tuck his shirt back into his slacks. Seemed like it happened every few days, but that was just his dumb luck, he told himself. He had always had such dumb luck. Like the time his robe flew open on Halloween, while opening the door for some local children. Or the handful of times he forgot to lock the men's room door back at the office, or at local restaurants and cafes. It seemed that dumb luck had conspired to reveal Burnam's penis to two or three hundred people over the years. Despite all the attendant risks, Burnam stretched and stretched high. The bus would be here any minute and he was exhausted from the last three days. All the planning, and preparing, and flying, and sleeping in the barracks- the private General's quarters, but still, barracks- had taken its toll on his old, withered frame. He hadn't had a good cup of coffee in almost 72 hours, to boot.

He stretched, and sure enough, his shirt became untucked and he waited to see if any subordinates would notice. They flitted around pressing buttons, checking cables and monitors, testing walkies, but none noticed the disheveled general waving his arms above his head.

The energy in the cavernous bunker was growing. The experiment would begin almost the moment the volunteers stepped off the bus. A few feet away Mehlman turned on a closed circuit monitor and the screen popped to life. Oh, great, Burnam thought. It's in black and white. All the closed circuit cameras transmitted in black and white, because color cost money, but logic doesn't temper complaints, because complainers complain, and Burnam was a chronic complainer.

"The eggplant gave me indigestion," he mewled at Mehlman. "Did the eggplant give you indigestion?"

Mehlman estimated he had answered hundreds of thousands of Burnam's minor concerns over the last thirty years: too few office supplies; the color of the drapes; so-and-so's attitude; sore feet; the receptionist's commitment to her job; the speed at which traffic lights change; military uniforms are too tight; too many Indian restaurants in California; and now, greasy eggplant.

"I have indigestion," said Mehlman, flatly. "But not from the eggplant."

He had learned that an exchange with Burnam was tolerable as long as he didn't have to look at the man, so Mehlman never made eye contact during these exchanges. In thirty years, he had made eye contact when responding to Burnam twice, and both times by accident. In a perfect world, Burnam would take the lack of eye contact as a signal that the person to whom he was complaining didn't want to be bothered, but that would require some humility, and some self-awareness, two traits that aging narcissists lack in spades. Mehlman's singular purpose over the last thirty years had been to retire, and he stared straight ahead, right down that tunnel into the dull grey light of obscurity, since the day he returned from The Shit, and to break away from his forward mission to answer Burnam's tripe about the new parking passes, or the "unfair" humidity had been- and would always be- anathema to him.

"Is that them?" asked Burnam.

"Who else would it be?"

"Do we just... start?"

"Hold on just one second, god damn it," barked Mehlman.

"I was just asking."

"As soon as the bus is..."

Mehlman and Burnam watched the bus reverse into the forest, the headlights suddenly swallowed by trees.

"Silvio, come show me how to use this thing," called Mehlman, and he pointed at the gray tabletop microphone in front of him.

A slim private, no more than 25 marched over to the control center. "Press here, speak, let go," he said dryly, like a child showing his father how to operate the television remote. Mehlman looked over the top of his glasses at the small black button that said, "TALK."

"And they'll hear me out there?" Mehlman asked, unconvinced.

"Yes," said Silvio, and then with meaning, "Sir."

"Thank you, Silvio, that'll be all."

Silvio hesitated before leaving, waiting for some other approval or gesture, but it never came. He turned on his heels and stomped away. Burnam watched the mise-en-scène with detachment. He had seen it before. Workplace flings were common and occasionally ugly.

Mehlman pressed the button and picked up a few pieces of paper from the desktop in front of him. The JAG's office had prepared a legal disclaimer for him to read. In the military, if you're read a disclaimer your consent is inferred, so this was a mere formality, but the military does formality well, and so Mehlman began.

"Welcome to Camp Wilikut," read Mehlman. He paused to watch the platoon's reaction, to make sure his voice was being heard. The hint of a smile crept over his face as the seven men turned and scanned for the origin of the voice in the sky.

*

"There!" shouted Richards.

Newman found the speaker and his stomach dropped. His hand shot up to his chest, to the photo of his girls. He felt around until he detected the edges of the photo. Suddenly he was tired, and embarrassed by his outward display of fear.

"Thank you for your participation," said the voice in the sky, and the tinny greeting ricocheted off the surrounding trees and flew down at them from every direction, deepening this hole in the woods. "The following test may gauge your olfactory response to any weapon in our non-lethal testing cache, including gas, odor, bacteria, and visual and/or audible cuing mechanisms, none of which are subject to FDA or FCC regulation, or have been deemed safe and/or legal by international treaty…"

The voice continued. Lincoln shook with fear at what he had just consented to by hearing the disclaimer. He could only envision hazed images of his own floundering death- when they say your imagination runs wild with the unknown, they don't mean you have one specific fear of possible torment that is fleshed out in detail and drilled down to the specific arc of infliction, pain, reaction, result… they mean that every possible iteration of every possible torture shoots through your consciousness in fractured images, out of order, bouncing between result and infliction, and pain and reaction, and at each image fracture your brain pauses and asks, could it be worse?, and if the answer is yes, your brain makes it worse, right there in the moment, to ensure you see the most absolutely horrific version of the potential infliction, pain, reaction or result, and this all happens thousands of times in a split second, until your heart pounds through your chest, your hands and feet become light as a feather in case you need to fight or flee, and, if you're like Andy Lincoln, you simultaneously lose all confidence in your own ability to do so. His arms and legs were cement, and he could do little but look to the others for some sort of direction.

Newman stared at the speaker. "…and should you attempt to do so, you may be shot on site, cremated, burned and disposed of at the military's discretion, on the basis of national security," said the voice in the sky. Newman swallowed hard.

"How do you turn this thing off," mumbled the voice. "Just let go," said another voice.

"Of what?"

"Just..."

With a click, the voice was gone. The men had been officially consented, and Newman demanded answers. More specifically, he needed directions.

"Do we just stand here then?" he yelled to the speaker.

Mehlman exhaled deeply, weeks of work had led to this moment, when the experiment would finally begin. He started to slide his chair away before he saw the man screaming up at him through at the closed circuit camera. Christ, thought Mehlman, it's always something. He peered over the top of his glasses and pressed the talk button.

"What?"

Newman was taken aback by this informal display of annoyance. He wasn't going to be bullied into complacency. He was a goddamn soldier, and soldiers needed orders, and they acted on those orders, and he wasn't about to just stand here with his thumb up his ass waiting around. "What the hell do you want us to do?" he shouted back at the speaker.

"What?" repeated Mehlman. He let go of the talk button. "Silvio!" he barked. "Silvio! How do I hear what the hell this guys is saying?"

Silvio sauntered over, irritated by the old man's oldness.

"We can't hear anything," he practically yawned the words out.

"What do you mean," growled Mehlman. Then, with meaning, "Private."

"We have no audio feed into the bunker," said Silvio. "Sir."

Newman thrust his hands onto his hips and looked around. Is nobody going to answer a one-star general, he thought? I got a stripe. I was in The Shit. I'm here giving my body to the United States of…"

"Sorry, gentlemen," came the voice in the sky. "Apparently, we don't have an audio feed into the bunker."

"What do you want us to do?" screamed Newman. "Blessed Mary, who is in charge of this clusterfuck?"

"Talking louder won't help," came the voice in the sky. "We can tell that you're yelling, but, again, we simply have no audio feed into the booth here. Do you understand? You could have a bullhorn and a full processional and we still couldn't hear you, okay?"

Newman began to yell back but caught himself. He was stumped. The men, exhausted, confused, shivering, simply stared at him. In a few swift seconds he had become their leader, by default perhaps, but still.

"Listen," came the voice in the sky, "I think I know what you're asking. Five clicks northwest, there is a suspected enemy encampment. Not a real one, mind you. One that we've set up. But treat it like a real one, will you? We want this to be as lifelike as possible. We will monitor your approach, disperse the O.C.D., and monitor your response. And then we'll all meet in the mess for dinner, assuming you, uh..." There was a pause.

"Godspeed," was all that followed.

Newman turned to face the men. He hadn't thought to take the reins, he had simply reacted to being abandoned, to being given no clear directive. Years of service had trained him to respond, to leave no ambiguity, to protect oneself against indecisive action, against stalling out. The men waited for him to speak.

"Uh," began Newman, drawing out the syllable while he searched for the words that would propel these men to… What? To be cannon fodder? Lab rats? Chemical sponges?

"Are they going to spray us with something?" cried Cruz. His tone sent a wave of panic through the men.

"They're just gonna shoot us," moaned Butterman.

"What?" cried Stryker. "They're gonna shoot us?"

"What is happening?" whined Lincoln.

"Just wait one god damn second," Newman barked over the moans of the group, but it was too late. Fear of the unknown had gripped the men and they spat terror all over each other.

"I can't do this," wailed Butterman. "They said I wasn't fit for field service, I got flat feet!"

"You think I want to be out here?" screamed Stryker. "It was either this or a court martial!"

"You, too?" asked James, the calmest of all.

"I needed the money," replied Lincoln.

Newman had had enough. "Now listen up, all of you!" he shouted.

"Who the hell are you?" shouted Stryker.

"Yeah," yelled Chico. "If you're such a bigshot, what are you doing here?"

Newman shifted his weight to his good knee. "I wanted to serve my country, one last time before…"

"Bullshit," said Stryker. "Nobody chooses to be a science experiment."

"Watch your mouth when you talk to a general, son!" barked Newman. He moved toward Stryker.

"You're not a general," screamed Stryker. "Out here you're a lab rat like everyone else!"

Newman was close enough to swing. "I'm the ranking officer, boy."

The men pulled them apart as Richards pleaded for calm. "We are out here as a unit!" he shouted. "Whether we like it or not!"

"He's right," said Private James. He held Stryker firmly by the arm, and his eyes told Stryker to respect the chain of command. Stryker relented, and twisted his arm free.

"Why are you here?" asked James.

Newman collected himself and smoothed his shirt. He stood up straight. He considered Private James, no more than 20, frightened, green. The authority had been solidified, not because Newman took it, but because the men gave it to him. They respected the stripes, if not yet the man who held them, and that type of authority was tenuous, and it would need to be renewed over and over again. He felt he must answer the question to let the men in, a little bit. Besides, the story ends in him whipping a young insubordinate, he thought. No harm in planting that seed.

"I'll tell you why I'm here, boys," he began, with just a hint of a growl, which he added for effect. "I…" He searched for the words. "I disciplined a boy under my command for insubordination."

"Disciplined?" asked Richards.

"I slapped him, and when he stood, I took his jaw in my hand and drove him into the wall," growled Newman. "And he called his daddy, and the boys upstairs went ape, and here I am."

The men stiffened. None of them had ever so much as shoved someone.

"This is your punishment?" asked Richards.

"This is my last best chance to serve," replied Newman, and he meant it.

Stryker broke the silence. "I didn't sign up to be slapped around by some washed up Patton," he snarled.

"Until this is over," snapped Richards, "or until that star comes off his shoulder, you will follow..." Richards read the name from just above Newman's breast pocket. "...General Ginger, and so will the rest of us."

As uncomfortable as Newman was with someone else forcing subordination upon the men, he gathered quickly that his only move was to keep quiet, to appear above the fray. He recalled a lesson he had learned early in the fatal chaos of the jungle: the more you have to tell people you're in charge, the less you're in charge. So he kept his mouth shut, gripped his hands behind his back, and began.

"Now, boys, if we're going in there, we're going in together, as a unit. We may be only seven-strong, but we're..." he paused and looked at the assembled men. How does one inspire the lame, he thought? How does one flatter the talentless? How does one spin? In the army, Newman remembered, you don't.

"Well, we're going in there because we have to," said Newman, with a new solemnity. "We're soldiers, and we have an order to follow. Could be marching to certain, immediate death..."

Over the last thirty years he had given one battle speech, to a group of engineers who were desperately trying to create a mechanism to improve the septic system on base. He had inspired the engineers by threatening that, if they failed, the base would be overrun with shit. It wasn't graceful, but it worked.

"Could be marching to slow, torturous death," he continued. "Maybe poison. Maybe mental anguish, confusion, deceit, trickery. Who knows? I don't. You certainly don't." Newman shifted uncomfortably now, his mind raced to find its point. "At the end of the day, you're still soldiers. And I am your general." He stopped and faced the men, and waited for eye contact from each. "And this is our war."

Chapter 7

Mehlman yawned and reclined in his captain's chair. He stroked the cracked brown leather and wondered how to sneak the chair out of the bunker and onto the plane home. He would have to disassemble it first. But that would draw attention. Perhaps he would have Silvio do it. The downside, of course, would be owing Silvio something, but that wasn't all bad.

He glanced across the bunker at Burnam, curled in the fetal position on his General's Cot, mandatory in all military bunkers following the '97 incident at Fort Meade where an exhausted general collapsed directly onto The Big Red Button- that Big Red Button- and almost started World War III. It had taken a diplomatic miracle, a handful of bribes, a renegotiation of trade rates and an official state visit to calm the reds after that one. Now there were cots. A small sign glued above the cots read, simply, "Naps Encouraged."

Mehlman wanted a nap but it was his shift. At his age, it was damn near impossible to make it past 10:00 pm, let alone pull an all-nighter. He had forced himself to suck down steaming cups of green tea and a half-dozen diet colas to arrive here, at 6:16 am, and he was barely coherent, but he was here. Despite needing to relieve himself every thirty minutes- thanks to the tea, the cola, and the enlarged prostate- he felt the slightest tinge of pride at his ability to hang with all these strapping, fresh young men. I still got it, he thought.

"Sir," barked one of the three lieutenants assigned to monitor the experiment, "we have movement on the northwest pitch."

"Fine, bring it up," said Mehlman. His central monitor flickered and through the predawn haze he could make out seven shapes wiggling through the tall grass toward the river. "E.T.A. at dispersion point?" he asked.

"Six minutes, sir."

*

Newman frantically waved the men forward. He could see the flickering lights of the enemy encampment in the distance and he knew it was critical they reach the camp before sunrise- even under the cover of this fog, the platoon would be at a substantial disadvantage if they waited to attack when the enemy was awake. The men crawled through the tall brush, toward the river, guns at the ready. The army had been kind enough to supply AK-47 rifles, to further simulate the textures of battle. Unfortunately, none of the men had held a gun recently enough to be effective with it, so the heavy, cold steel had the exact opposite of its intended effect- the platoon was just as frightened of their own weapons as they were of the enemy's.

Fear turned to terror as nothing happened. Dreadful scenarios played themselves out in each man's mind; snapshots of torture, of violent, bloody deaths, wailing and spasms flickered in front of each man's eyes. The ambient buzz of the forest and the river created an unrelenting soundtrack of pure pitch, a nagging squeal that barely ebbed enough every few minutes to let the men breathe. The cacophony would swell and just at the moment it should explode into silence, it would ease, and begin again. There was no release, there was no climax, there was no end. There was only the ebb, and the flow. The men crawled forward, toward the river, and prayed for something- a gunshot, an explosion, a war cry to signal they'd been spotted and the battle must start- but it would not come.

Newman felt a break in the rhythm of the platoon. He propped himself up on his elbow and raised his other hand, straight and tall. He felt the men stop around him, yet there it was, a movement out of sync with the flock. It came from the left wing, thirty meters southwest. He clumsily turned on his elbows, shifting an inch here and an inch there, and peered through the site on his rifle.

Behind a tree just beyond the wood line, a shape shifted. In this light, he couldn't discern the form- could be a bear, could be a mountain cat, could be a gook, he thought. He used "gook" as a shorthand for "enemy" in his own mind, knowing that the term had become politically incorrect almost the moment he returned from The Shit. The American Public was more than willing to let you kill a bunch of gooks but the moment you called them gooks, all of a sudden you were a monster. But he wasn't a monster. The last action he saw was 'Nam, the last men he killed were gooks, and in order to forgive himself for the killings he had decided long ago to believe the Vietnamese were and always would be evil, and thinking of them as "gooks" was not only helpful but necessary to maintain the illusion and keep the truce with himself.

Through his site Newman made out the shape of a gun. His eyes went wide as saucers. So this was it? They were going to be fired upon from the flanks, he thought? It was uninspired, but what a goddamn relief, he thought! Newman leapt to his feet. Before the men could react he had the rifle butt firmly lodged in his right shoulder, his right index finger on the trigger, right eye three inches from the site. His form came rushing back to him, he was 23 again, every muscle tweaked and tightened. The platoon watched, horrified. Soldiers in name only, they had been collectively praying for some sort of psychological test. In theory, they should have jumped to their feet and fallen in behind General Ginger but they instead hunkered lower into the grass and said a silent prayer that whatever was behind that tree had excellent aim and zero bloodlust.

The figure picked up its gun and instinctively Newman fired. The shots exploded out of the muzzle in rapid succession, tiny bursts of orange and red fire peeking through the grey fog. There was a scream from the direction of the figure. Newman's chest nearly exploded with the excitement of a kill, he couldn't think, he couldn't hear. He sprinted toward the figure behind the tree.

Richards leapt to his feet and dropped his gun. It was heavy and dangerous and he couldn't for the life of him figure out how to run with it. He sprinted after Newman, determined to help broker a peace deal with the enemy or perform CPR on the old man should his heart quit on him.

Newman was thirty feet from the tree and closing. He let out a guttural cry and raised his gun, just as the figure leapt out from behind the tree and let out his own guttural cry, slightly higher in pitch than Newman's. His gun was propped against his stomach and he fired directly into Newman's chest. Newman froze. The gunman released the trigger and the fireworks stopped.

Private First Class Dwight Butterman stood fifteen feet away, his pants around his ankles, an AK-47 aimed straight at the general. Newman felt his abdomen for hot, sticky blood and spilled guts. Why didn't he feel anything? Was this death? Sudden and numbing?

Richards ran to the scene and stopped. "Hold your fire!"

"Butterman," Newman screamed. "What the hell are you doing out of formation?"

"I had to pee," whispered Butterman.

Richards' eyes darted between the two men, who should've been ripped to shreds by each other's bullets. The three men looked at the guns.

"Blanks," mumbled Richards.

"If this was live," said Butterman, in shock, "you would'a killed me."

"If this was live, you'd be dead weight on the entire platoon," growled Newman. "And it wouldn't be me that killed you, it'd be your own goddamn selfishness. I'd pull the trigger, but it was your selfishness put you in front of the gun. Of course, I'd be dead or court martialed, then all these boys would'a been under the leadership of who?"

Richards and Butterman looked to each other, overwhelmed by the mental exercise coming so hard on the heels of a near-death experience.

"Exactly. Nobody. You exposed yourself to the enemy, you exposed our position to the enemy, and now your platoon is without a leader, five men against the world, and you're dead and I'm in jail, all because you got a bitch's bladder and you're too goddamn precious to piss your pants like a real man."

Newman paused and waited for a response on the off-chance that ol' Deadweight had something intelligent to say, but true to form, thought Newman, this asshole is just gonna stand there with his mouth open, waiting for someone to shove a hotdog in. "Do you have anything to say for yourself?"

"I had to pee," stammered Butterman.

Unimpressed, Newman turned and started to march back to the stunned men, still cowering in the tall grass. He felt good. Leading a platoon was sort of like riding a bike, he thought. I mean, sure, two-sevenths of the platoon would be dead if this simulation was real, but I was right, he thought. I had been firm but fair, and ol' Deadweight surely won't make the same mistake again. And isn't that what leadership is about, he thought? Adapting and improvising, learning from mistakes, teaching…

"Asshole," grumbled Butterman, just loud enough.

Newman stopped. "Excuse me, private?"

"You don't have to be an asshole, man," said Butterman, losing confidence with each word.

Newman turned back to Butterman and marched to within an inch of the frightened young man's soft, round face.

"Yes, I do," he growled. "Deadweight."

Butterman looked at the ground, terrified. He was in over his head, and he knew it.

Inside the bunker, Mehlman grew impatient. "General Burnam, get over here and press this god-damn button."

Burnam rolled off his cot and tucked his erection behind his belt buckle, a trick he had mastered in his school days, when one could be called to stand and answer a question, or write on the chalkbaord at any moment. This one had burst forth during his nap, thanks to a luscious dream starring a petite Spaniard and a beach somewhere in the tropics. "Where are they?"

"Close enough," said Mehlman.

Newman pressed closer to Deadweight's face. "I don't give a fuck about your precious feelings. I'm here to get you out of The Shit alive. You wanna complain that the big, mean general hurt your feelings when he yelled at you? Call your mama, boy. This is war."

"Delivering the O.C.D.," said Burnam.

"Go for O.C.D.," acknowledged Mehlman.

Burnam pressed the small red button labeled "INITIATE," just below the bank of monitors.

Newman leaned in and closed the last centimeters between him and Deadweight. "Do you underst…"

Three quick pops broke the ambient hum of the forest. Newman looked and saw three trails of purple smoke emanating from the enemy encampment ripping through the fog.

"Incoming!" screamed Cruz.

"Incoming! Incoming!" called the rest of the platoon.

"To the river!" screamed Newman. "To the river!"

The men threw their guns to the ground and sprinted toward the shallow river just ahead. Someone screamed. Someone recited the Lord's Prayer. Newman, still spry, sprinted ahead of the paunchy, slovenly men in their ill-fitting uniforms, determined to lead them into whatever fate awaited. He raised his gun above his head and let out an unbroken war cry as he closed on the river, but the whistle of the canisters drowned it out as they arced through the fog and purple smoke engulfed the sky. He dove head first into the river and the men followed, tumbling and splashing like frightened seals before a slaughter.

The first two canisters plunged into the water on either side of the platoon, but the third tore through the center of the icy river and crashed directly into Newman's nose, shattering it instantly. He felt the impact and thrashed in the water, terrified something had latched onto his face, and leapt to his feet, swinging wildly. Suddenly the dull throb raced to the bridge of his nose, his eyes swelled and he became dizzy with pain. He looked down at the river rippling past his thighs and could make out blood being washed away. He felt the phantom canister squeezing the bones in his face together, jamming his nose back into his eye sockets, and scooped some of the river with his cupped hands and splashed the water onto his nose. The sting was excruciating, but he did it again, hoping to numb the pain. Everything ached as purple gas swirled around him. He was disoriented and for a second he thought he was choking to death on the gas whatever it was, but he forced himself to find his breath. Calm yourself, he thought. Calm yourself down, goddamn it. You are a leader of men.

Newman turned to look for his boys through the purple haze. He ripped off his shirt and balled it up against what was left of his nose.

There was a break in the haze ten meters in front of him. He could make out the shape of another shirtless man- one of his boys, thank god. It was Richards, the wide-eyed kid. "Are you hit?" Newman screamed. "I think I broke my nose! God bless America, that smarts!"

There was no answer. Richards stared back at the general, silently, like a ghost, unaffected by the tide or the haze or anything else really, just watching, waiting.

Newman assumed Richards hadn't heard him, or perhaps was in shock. Perhaps this purple gas had muted him or temporarily turned him off. "I got it pretty good," he continued. "Right in the ol' sniffer! Hell of a shot, by god. Hell of a shot."

The haze began to dissipate and hints of the river crept through. In the distance Newman could make out another of his boys, the fat one, Deadweight. He was shirtless, for some reason, and standing like a goddamn zombie some twenty meters to the west. Then, on the other flank, downriver, some thirty meters east, Newman could see the Hispanic one, Cruz. He rose from the water slowly, like it was his first time standing in this world and the water rolled down his shirtless body. What in the bloody hell, thought Newman? Everybody lost their shirts? Suddenly, some twenty meters south, the last bits of haze cleared and Newman could see

Private First Class, Lamar James begin to emerge. Thank god, thought Newman, that's five. His relief turned to horror at the sight of James' flaccid penis, as he emerged from the river stark naked.

Newman's hand fell from his face, blood caked on his mouth and chest, on the rag in his hand and up and down his arms. These boys have gone native on me, he thought. He desperately wanted the exercise to end, for someone to blow a whistle or ring a bell, gather them all back up and dump them on a bus home. These boys are zombies, a bunch of naked zombies staring at me, he thought, and suddenly he didn't want to be the general anymore. Suddenly he was a terrified private, surrounded by people who were not well, and not listening.

Lincoln stood, completely naked, his small, thin body almost childlike next to the sturdy James. Newman turned to Richards, still frozen only a few meters away.

"Where's your shirt, soldier?" he asked. It was the best he could do. He knew, not so deep down, that Richards had no idea where his shirt went, nor did he care. Even while he asked the question, he knew he would get no answer, because something had shifted in the world. As the haze lifted, it took some piece of reality with it, some component of life on earth, and now the world, which had been consistently marching straight through space and time along its predictable trajectory at its predictable speed, had… Stopped.

The low, constant rattle and hum of the world moving forward had a way of lulling a man to sleep, and Newman suddenly felt very awake, and he didn't like it. The future, at least the near future, had been carried into the ether with the purple haze, a curtain lifted to reveal a new world in place of the old one, identical save for the energy between the players.

Newman suddenly felt very, very alone. If he was in a new world, these men were in a new universe. It was as if they had emerged from the river as a new species. He took a quick count- five- one man unaccounted for. His eyes sprang wildly from man to man but he couldn't move. These men would catch him if he ran, he knew. They would pummel him, they would kill him, they would eat him. He was so transfixed on the men in front of him he did not think to look behind him. Stryker, thin as a rail and naked as the day he was born grew from the water just a few feet behind Newman. Newman sensed the movement, and listened for malice, or speed, but none came, only heat. Without warning Richards and Stryker began to drift silently toward him and he flushed red, and adrenaline tore through his muscles and chest. In the distance he could see James and Lincoln embrace, and Deadweight began to wade downriver to Cruz. Richards and Stryker were feet away when Lincoln and James kissed for the first time. Newman felt faint. He saw Deadweight reach Cruz and the two men embraced like long parted lovers. These men, these soft, weak castaways who were moments from crumbling into dirt were suddenly standing, fearless, passionate... Newman suddenly felt the current, felt the water against his legs as his brain begged his body to collapse, just collapse and let the river drag you away, he thought. He reached into the water for the gun strapped to his ankle, a pistol he pulled on every morning same as socks, but his eyes quit and his head spun and there was water everywhere and black, thank God.

*

Mehlman reclined in his captain's chair with his arms crossed over his chest, bored but grateful this ordeal was almost over. He stared at the central monitor, which appeared to be one large grey blob. They saw the men dive into the river, and they saw the OCD canisters streak past the cameras, but within seconds of delivery their view had been wiped out by the haze, and they'd been flying blind for almost two minutes now.

Though this was his first, it seemed to Mehlman that in the world of human science experiments two minutes must be an eternity. Their faces could be melted off by now, he thought. They could be drowning, or gutting each other. We need a giant box fan to expedite this haze, he thought. Do we have a giant box fan? He chuckled to himself at the thought of a box fan the size of a small cottage, blowing trees over and whipping men around like leaves. Now, that is a weapon the boys upstairs should experiment with, he thought. None of this mamby-pamby chemical shit. This is America, goddamnit. The Wind Blaster. A box fan powerful enough to blow men down a street like tumbleweeds. This is good, he thought. But why stop there? Why not make it powerful enough to reject bullets? Or missiles? If you could flip a switch on the Blaster and deflect enemy bullets back onto the enemy, you wouldn't need bullets of your own. Can you imagine how much money the U.S. military would save if they never needed bullets again?

Mehlman was getting excited. He pulled the napkin from under his mug and a pen from his breast pocket. He scribbled down "MASSIVE BOX" at the top of the napkin and began to sketch a demo beneath: a big square with four curved blades on the left side of the napkin and on the right, he sketched a slew of stick figures being blown willy-nilly. He knew he had to add movement, so he sketched three lines extending between the fan and the stick figures. When he was done he shook with excitement.

Burnam glanced over. He was awake, barely, but Mehlman's jittering had kept him alert for the past few minutes. He peeked over Mehlman's shoulder but couldn't make out the sketch. The poor man has been awake for almost 24 hours, thought Burnam, he's probably punch-drunk. Neither man noticed the haze begin to clear from in front of the closed circuit camera lens. Blurred heads and shirtless bodies began to appear onscreen. Chilled, panicked whispers shot through the bunker, as the research team scribbled furious notes and pressed button after button to ensure this was being properly monitored and recorded.

Burnam leaned forward casually and tried to get a better view of the general's napkin, but Mehlman sensed him and shifted his shoulders ever so slightly to protect his baby. "What?" asked Burnam defensively.

"Don't 'what' me," snipped Mehlman.

On the monitor the haze had all but disappeared, and two men appeared to wrestle naked in the river, while a shirtless man sprinted out of view. Phones began to chirp. Techies began to scurry about the room.

"I'm a good drawer, I could help you."

"I don't need your help," barked Mehlman. "You've been helping me for 30 years, look where it got us."

Noticing the bustle around them, both men reflexively looked to the center monitor. There, in black and white, three pair of naked men made what could only be described as- even upon first glance- passionate, sensual love.

"No," whispered Mehlman.

"Dear god," whispered Burnam.

"Sir?" offered a timid grunt from a nearby bank of monitors, but neither general could hear him. The world had come to a screeching halt, and though the world stopped, the screeching continued.

Mehlman felt a tingling in his neck. Suddenly his left hand was numb, gone. A tourniquet wrapped around the veins in his arm and the left side of his body weighed a thousand pounds.

"Deichmann!" screamed Burnam. "Are you seeing this?" He pointed to the bank of monitors, eleven televisions filled with various views of grainy, black and white man-on-man intercourse.

Friedrich Deichmann lifted a trembling cup of coffee to his lips and took a tortured sip. "Seeing what?" he said, in as casual a voice as he could muster. Deichmann was small and stout, and had a full head of grey-white hair, tousled in every direction. He wore his lab coat everywhere, which gave the impression of authority and calm, but at the moment his shaking hands dribbled piping hot coffee all over themselves.

"Damn it man, get over here!" shouted Burnam.

"Okay," said Deichmann, though he didn't move.

"Now!" screamed Burnam.

Deichmann shuffled across the bunker and leaned a little too far into the bank of monitors, attempting to prove that he didn't know what he would see. "Oh my," he offered.

"This was not part of the plan, doctor!"

"Hmm."

"What?"

"Yes, interesting."

"What is interesting?"

"The current outcome," stammered Deichmann, "is certainly… interesting."

"How could this happen?" screamed Burnam. He grew tired. Perhaps this was a dream, he thought. And where the hell was Mehlman? Why was he so goddamn quiet?

"The Orbito-Frontal Cortex, the center of all human arousal," pleaded Deichmann. "By stimulating the O.F.C. directly we circumvent any inhibitions the brain may offer when faced with arousal."

"What arousal?" cried Burnam. "They're a bunch of young soldiers swimming shirtless in a stream! Who could that possibly arouse?"

"The human body's reception of any stimulant is difficult to predict at best," floundered Deichmann.

Burnam waved his hand to silence the scientist. All this scientific jibber-jabber only frustrated him. Sounded like a whole bunch of space talk, a fancy way to say nothing. He began to panic. This was not one of those sign-and-seal deals, this was some type of serious shitbag. It would be one thing if these louts had sucked down the gas and emerged from the river with a blood-lust or some kind of wobbly insanity, that would be fine, expected even. We've been gassing test subjects for decades, watching them kill themselves, or each other, he thought. But these men emerged from the river, and began to… *make love.* Heads were going to roll.

As Black Ops edged toward the platoon on the monitors, Burnam turned to Mehlman, who had been surprisingly silent throughout this ordeal. "Well?" asked Burnam. But no answer came. Mehlman was slumped back in his seat, a vague, distant look nailed to his face, as if frozen in place while recalling a painful memory, or a whole lifetime of them. The black ops pulled one man from the river and crept toward the distracted couplings as Burnam prodded Mehlman. "Barry?"

But Barry Mehlman was dead, and Deichmann knew it. He watched Burnam shrink from his dead friend and mentor, and he watched the black ops close in on the platoon, and he felt the stunned silence of the young techs and grunts around him, and he realized that life, at least for him and probably a few dozen other men, had just taken one of those fabled turns, and heads were most certainly going to roll.

Chapter 8

Burnam and Deichmann shifted in their seats. Fuller had not said a word since the filmstrip began. When he received the initial reports, he imagined there was a plausible spin somewhere. He imagined there would be ambiguity, or things on screen that could be mistaken for something else, or placed in a different context, or there were simple *inconclusivities*- a word he had coined back when he was investigating war crimes in The Shit and had urged the JAG's office to adopt. But there were no inconclusivities on this reel, there was no difficult context, there was only men joyfully and grandly making love to other men. Fuller's gut told him the proverbial shit was going to hit the proverbial fan. He took a drag on his cigarette- he found he was smoking more now, ever since the news came back, first, in panicked shouts over the phone, and then hysterical briefs in person, and finally now, on film, an indisputable, iron-clad recordation that was immune to human misinterpretation. He scratched his pockmarked face and leaned back in his chair, it was not his style to reveal his hand, he kept a poker face and wore disinterest the way powerful men do, even though inside there was very distinctly a knot or some such tumor forming in his belly.

Burnam began to stammer, "There could potentially be some inconclus…"

"Looks pretty gay to me," interrupted Fuller.

"Well," stammered Burnam, "We didn't ask."

"And they didn't tell," added Deichmann. His concern for the subjects and their safety had grown in the 48 hours since they were removed from Camp Wilikut. He had not been allowed to see them and nobody would tell him their whereabouts. He knew they were alive because the military would want to come to some understanding of how this happened, and whether the technology was in some way useful, so they would, for the time being take reasonable care of the subjects.

"Where are they now?" asked Fuller.

"Quarantined," said Burnam, with a look to Deichmann, who he knew itched for a real answer.

"Are we worried about it spreading?" asked Fuller.

"Pardon?" asked Deichmann, not quite sure he had heard the general correctly.

"Is it contagious?" said Fuller.

Deichmann was about to answer in the negative, but, and this was rare for Deichmann, he first asked himself what answer would best serve his purposes. He did some quick calculations and came up with the one answer that would get him closer to the men sooner, so he could get back to work. "That is an inconclusivity, sir," he said. As a doctor, he prided himself on frankness, on a lack of ulterior motive in his answers, but he had engineered this study and with every passing hour he was losing extraordinary amounts of invaluable data. His manipulation paid off. Fuller turned his head ever so slightly, peering in the general direction of Deichmann with a raised eyebrow. From a stone wall like Fuller, this was a grand tell, the word had stuck, and Deichmann felt a tinge of hope for the first time in almost two days.

"No chance of reversing this?" asked Fuller.

"Not without removing their Orbito-Frontal Cortex in its entirety," said Deichmann, "an extremely complicated proced…"

"Their orbito-what-now?" interrupted Fuller.

"They would need lobotomies, sir," said Deichmann.

"Sounds expensive."

"It would be expensive, sir."

"Do we need to cordon them off from one another? So they don't…" Fuller's voice trailed off as he searched for the words. Finally he took his right index finger and pulsed it in and out through a left-handed "okay" symbol several times.

"They're not rabbits, sir," said Deichmann.

Before Fuller could respond, a young aide popped his head into the screening room. "He's ready for you, sir," he whispered. Deichmann was concerned by the nervous excitement in the aide's voice. Who was this he, and why were they going to speak with him? Another layer of bureaucracy meant another round of explanations and manipulations, even more hours away from the test subjects, more knowledge lost, evaporated into the ether of wasted time.

Before he knew it they were marching down one hallway, then another, and another, and another. For all he could tell they were walking in giant circles around what felt like the world's largest office building.

The aide practically skipped he was so excited as he led them through the endless hallways, and Fuller and Burnam marched hard on his heels. Deichmann, used to a stationary life on a lab stool, had to jog to keep pace. "General Burnam," he asked, "where are we going?"

"To see the Secretary of Defense," he replied. "Of the United States of America."

*

Deichmann could feel beads of sweat collecting on his lower back and around his collar. It hit like a thunderclap, where they were- the six hour flight, the midnight caravan, the never-ending hallways... Following the disastrous experiment in the woods, the two surviving members of the implementation team had been shuttled across the country to Washington, D.C., to the Pentagon, the beating heart of United States military operations around the world.

They were ushered into a reasonable office and they took their seats in three plush chairs across from a desk where a man with white hair sat with his back to them. Deichmann thought it bizarre because there was no window to peer out of, there was only a wall with a few plaques and a large, generic painting of a foxhunt, and the white haired man didn't appear to be staring at that even, but at some bare patch of wall. He felt Burnam tense up, could see the man's spine stiffen and eyes widen, and after a quick glance around the room he saw the thing that had given Burnam the palpitations, though he did not understand why: in the back of the room sat a congenial looking fellow, legs crossed, patiently watching. The name on his uniform read "Howell."

The white haired man in the chair must have sensed that everyone was seated, because he slowly spun around in his chair to face the small group. His double chin spilled over the tightly buttoned collar and onto the four stars on each lapel of his dress uniform, and Deichmann noted this was the only thing about Secretary of Defense William "Chick" Cadbury that was not immaculate. The room was immaculate, his highly decorated dress uniform was immaculate, even the corners of Cadbury's face around and above the chin, and the tightly quaffed white hair was immaculate, but as Cadbury reclined, that jowly double chin popped out like some repository for all the fat that was simply not allowed by army regulations to collect elsewhere.

Cadbury was not impressed with the two new faces before him. Howell and Fuller he knew, they were company men, career men, and the good thing about career men is you don't have to explain yourself to career men. You tell them to do the thing, the thing gets done, because career men look up, not out. Cadbury often equated it- in his mind, of course, never out loud- to having young children or dogs. They value your approval over God's- for them, you are God- and that's exactly what makes them so valuable to a man in authority. As for these other two assholes, Cadbury was unsettled. They could be dimwits who were given the wheel and through sheer stupidity drove the bus off a cliff, or they could be treacherous pranksters who took the wheel in order to drive it off the cliff, there was no way to know. This uncertainty left Cadbury on uneven footing. Was he looking at monsters or fools? Or both?

He looked at the two men for the first time, studied them. They were sweating profusely. Cadbury began to lean toward "fools." Yes, they must be fools because if they had any guile they would've been promoted long ago, they would've become career men. These guileless fools were assigned this task in the first place because they were dispensable, because a week spent on a useless perfume bomb wouldn't detract from some other more meaningful pursuit like miniaturizing nuclear weapons, or training dolphins to suicide bomb enemy submarines, both close to Cadbury's heart. Yes, these men were fools.

"Indulge me doctor," he began. "As a man of science, surely you must have a philosophy about the question of what separates man from beast."

"Well, yes," shook Deichmann. "There is only one thing really."

"Opposable thumbs?" blurted Fuller.

"Valiant effort, General Fuller," said Cadbury.

"I was referring to our powers of reason, sir," said Deichmann.

"It is true, doctor. Some people believe our great powers of reason are what separate us from the beasts," said Cadbury. After a short pause, he added, "Nonsense."

Deichmann felt a ball of phlegm forming in his throat that was desperate to escape, to climb into his mouth and gum up the works. He swallowed hard.

"Eroticism, doctor. Eroticism is what separates man from beast. The pursuit of pleasure for some end other than reproduction," continued Cadbury.

"Fucking, for fucking's sake. Animals fuck to survive, doctor. We fuck for sport. And the greatest perpetuators of this insidious eroticism?" Cadbury looked directly into the doctor's eyes, this would be the moment that told Cadbury if he was truly staring into the eyes of a fool or a traitor. "Do you know, doctor, who are the greatest perpetrators of this insidious eroticism?" The doctor appeared clueless. Cadbury was a touch disappointed.

"Homosexuals," he practically spat the word at Deichmann. "The gravest threat to mankind's survival since influenza. If carried out to its ultimate end, widespread homosexuality is no longer a passive indulgence but an active betrayer of the human reproductive cycle, with the ability to end the propagation of the entire human race. I'm talking about the end of civilization, doctor." He took a second to show reflection, to shake his head to remind everyone in the room just how serious the end of civilization would be.

"When you think about it in those terms, weaponized homosexuality was an inevitability," he continued. "Thank God the American military got there first: we can rest assured this awesome power will be handled with awesome discretion." Deichmann could feel himself shrinking. "After all, man must fiercely protect his rather conditional place on this earth. Animals, on the other hand, predate man, and they will be here long after we're gone, for one reason: there are no homosexual animals. That's a fact. Despite the potential for fleeting, erotic bliss, animals choose heterosexuality exclusively, and therefore, God's light will shine upon them in perpetuity. So, I ask you, doctor, who has the greater powers of reason? Us, or the beasts?"

Deichmann could not be sure if the stunned silence was shared amongst the group, he only knew his mouth no longer worked. Neither did his arms, or legs, or neck. He couldn't even lift his eyes from the middle of Cadbury's desk, let alone form an answer to one of the most complex questions of life on earth. He was in a waking coma, he thought. Life will continue to swirl about me and I will be glued here in living rigor mortis, watching others take what is mine.

Fuller broke the silence. "What are you suggesting we do with them, sir?"

"Who?" asked Cadbury.

"The platoon, sir."

"They are quarantined currently?"

"Barracks 175, sir."

"How many people know about this?"

"Outside of this room, sir? No one."

"Burn the barracks to the ground."

At this, Deichmann sprang to life. "May I suggest rigorous testing?" he pleaded. "An empirical evaluation of any unintended side effects?" His arms and legs felt heavy, bogged down in quicksand, but at least he was alive, he thought, not dead... yet.

"Side effects?" asked Cadbury. "Like what?"

"Like lisps," sneered Fuller.

"Like infections, or chronic illnesses that may emerge over time. We don't even know the permanence of the homosexuality…"

"Do we need to?" interrupted Cadbury. "If word of this catastrophe spreads we will become the laughing-stock of the entire armed world."

"Unless our tests reveal some practical application of their talents," begged Deichmann.

"Yeah," laughed Fuller. "I bet they put on a fabulous cabaret act. Maybe we can loan them out to the U.S.O."

Deichmann ignored the bait. Though his legs would not push him there, he had managed to pull himself to the edge of his chair. "Sir?"

Cadbury studied him. Perhaps this doctor was not such a fool after all.

Chapter 9

"Sec Def himself has asked me to test your strength, speed, agility, endurance and accuracy with a firearm," barked the drill sergeant, a viciously erect, mustached, oak of a man. He paced back and forth some twenty meters away from the assembled platoon. "They did not mention I'd be testing a bunch of prancing faggots."

The bitter, squinting expression Newman wore in professional settings drained from his face. He could feel his usually stiff spine wilt. It was the first time in his long life that he had been called a faggot, and the show of veteran strength and fortitude he had planned for the sergeant and the platoon today dissolved instantly. The dull throb behind his nose and eyes had returned and he rubbed the flimsy bandage for relief. He was forced to apply it himself, a hackneyed, cockeyed composite of broken tongue depressors and band-aids, pieced together from the barracks first aid kit.

Aside from the MRE's delivered three times daily, the platoon had had no contact with the outside world. Even the MRE's were dropped just inside the newly constructed fence surrounding their barracks, then an air horn was blown and the platoon was allowed to enter the field and pick up their powdered and flattened meals.

"Field" was a generous term for the ten-foot dirt patch between the barracks door and the fence, and "fence" was a generous term for the thin steel poles mounted in small concrete cubes with chain link between them. The men could have easily toppled it, but never would- they were soldiers, and they understood a direct order even when it was delivered passive aggressively (they awoke on their first morning to find the fence had been constructed overnight, while they slept).

The fence was built, in a sense, for their own protection, as there were armed guards, instructed to shoot to kill, positioned in small watchtowers at all four corners of the barracks. The watchtowers could not be built overnight, so instead they were bought. Three base grunts were sent to a local fish and game store, but were turned away because the season's deer blinds were long sold out. The owner suggested a nearby outdoor furniture store, The Gazebo Glen, where four children's tree houses were purchased, loaded onto a flatbed and brought back to base. The platoon climbed onto beds and watched through the tiny windows above every other bunk as the tree houses were driven into view and, over the course of eight hours, carefully maneuvered off the flatbeds and into position by a team of twelve or so. Though the snipers were hesitant at first they eventually had a laugh and helped construct their perches before climbing in.

In the 72 hours since the experiment the men had undergone some startling changes. All except Newman, whose only development was the black and blue bruising around his nose and under each eye, courtesy of the projectile that smashed into his face. That was the last coherent memory Newman retained from the experiment. He could see flashes of other things, horrific things he was grateful to forget, but the crack of the metal canister against the bone and the audible crunch that followed still rang through his head. The pounding was most excruciating when he was forced to look at the men, when one engaged him in conversation, or passed him on the way to and from the shitter.

Richards, on the other hand, had grown by three inches and almost twenty pounds. His muscles bulged from under the very same uniform that hung off his shoulders just days ago. He had shaved his floppy, criss-crossed hair to within an inch of his scalp and had developed a light tan where once pale, loose skin hung. His voice was not an octave lower but his words were suddenly delivered with such quiet confidence it might as well have been.

As for Lincoln, he could see, suddenly, without glasses, and his pigeon foot had straightened itself out overnight, and for the first time in his life he could walk in a straight line. He wept to himself at the memory of being tormented as a boy for always drifting right. A race would break out between boys, as it often does when there are boys, a field, and spare time, and young Andy Lincoln would bolt into the game like any good boy. No matter how close he stood to the other boys at the beginning of the race, invariably he ended up meters and meters away, or worse, flat on his face because that god damn pigeon foot simply could not propel itself upward and forward at the same rate as his properly aligned foot.

Stryker's skin had cleared up, and his gaunt, sunken eyes were suddenly forward and vibrant. James's belly had disappeared and was replaced with visible, defined auburn-brown abdominal muscles, and his glasses became redundant when he, too, awoke on the second morning with 20/20 vision.

Cruz's teeth straightened themselves and his posture and grammar improved dramatically. He found he was a little more optimistic even. He was always a cheerful guy, but now he meant it. His cheer wasn't hope, it was genuine and present.

Deadweight seemed to have the least noticeable change, next to Newman of course, who seemed not to have changed at all. Deadweight's hair was certainly less matted, and he thought he had sweated significantly less in the last three days than in any three-day stretch he could recall. It was easier to sit and stand, he noticed. His legs and back didn't ache for minutes after each exertion, like usual. All in all, if this was the only side effect of the experiment, he decided, he'd call it a success. Well, he'd call it a success, with one exception. There was still the matter of his sudden, inexplicable attraction to other men. He took solace in the knowledge that six of the seven men involved in the experiment experienced an immediate and profound desire to make love to another man, and had acted on it. He also took solace in the general's denial of the profound change, as it meant there was still hope that none of this was real, or if it was real, perhaps not permanent. Each man felt this same whiplashed confusion to varying degrees, and bounced between desperate bargaining and breathless anger from minute to minute.

The new gifts were small comfort, to all but Richards. Richards was satisfied to serve, in any capacity, and he hoped to keep his new weight, strength and confidence. In fact he was determined to do so. Though it came at a price, of course, he would gladly trade women for military talent, if that was the deal. His father was a soldier, and his father before him, and his father, and so on. The Richards clan was a warrior clan, and James Richards, the youngest of three boys in the service, was in the clan by birth, but not yet by deed. He had long hoped to spark to service, and assumed that spark would ignite either a talent or a passion strong enough to compensate for his lack of talent. He had spent the last 19 years on the outside looking in. Whatever this was, he decided, he was going to keep it, and use it.

"My duty is to God first, then country," said the sergeant, "so naturally I felt not too small a conflict in coming out here to administer said tests. However, I took comfort in knowing that when given a gun, most homos are so hot for the heavy, black steel in their hands they don't know whether to shoot it or jack it off. Therefore, based on entertainment value alone, I believe God will surely understand why I chose to come out here today." He stopped and faced the men for the first time. "Here is a hint: your gun will not ejaculate, no matter how fast you rub it."

"How do you know?" asked Stryker, to the astonishment and horror of the group.

The sergeant turned casually on his heels to face Stryker, whose smooth, tan skin and newly taut muscles had come with another side effect: hubris.

"What is your name, soldier?" asked the sergeant.

"Stryker," he purred.

"Son, that is the single gayest name I have ever heard."

"It's not half as bad as my nickname," teased Stryker.

"Stryker!" yelled Richards, through clenched teeth.

"What is your nickname, son?" growled the sergeant.

"My friends call me Stirrups," he said with a wink.

"I shudder to think what heinous sex act that nickname derives from, soldier," said the sergeant.

The rest of the platoon wasn't so worried about the origin of the name, because they knew the truth: nobody had touched anybody else, not so much as a hug, or a high-five since the day of the experiment. In fact, each man clung to this as potentially a sign that they could, somehow, at some point return to the person they had known themselves to be for the last couple of decades. Stryker, or Stirrups, or whatever the hell he wanted to be called had apparently decided instead to simply run with it, much to the delight of the sergeant, it appeared.

"Stirrups," he growled. He rolled it around on his tongue, "Stirrrups." Stirrups' smile slowly turned down as the sergeant refused to take the bait. The more the sergeant said the name- and appeared to enjoy saying the name- the more Stirrups became convinced he was in deep, deep shit.

"Stirrupsss," said the sergeant, hissing the final letters toward the stunned soldier. The sergeant then caught Lamar's eye despite his best effort to stand completely still, without so much as an unnecessary breath. Lamar had been bullied in middle and high school and had never forgotten the golden rule: avoid eye contact at all costs, and when that fails, simply avoid. He had walked out of class, into lockers, off curbs, and into traffic to avoid bullies before, but he could see the strategically placed tree houses just a few hundred meters away, a grim reminder that going AWOL was not an option. His new muscles felt explosive, but he was not about to test drive them now. "You poor bastard," lamented the sergeant. He looked Lamar up and down. "We'll call you, Two Strikes." The sergeant lingered for a second and watched realization creep over Lamar's face.

Newman was desperate to speak. If only he could get the sergeant alone, swap a couple war stories and level with him about this huge misunderstanding. Newman was a one star general, after all, and he was taking orders from a drill sergeant? If he could just pull him aside, or even interject with a quick introduction, he could explain everything. While the rest of the men stood stone still, praying that somehow this made them either invisible or boring to the sergeant, Newman leaned forward and called the sergeant over with slight, tweaking head nods and frantic eye rolls.

"If it isn't the soldier that time forgot," snarled the sergeant. Newman tried to speak but the sergeant was too quick and far too loud for Newman in this beaten and hazy state.

"Quit drooling, old man! If I wanted to take it in the ass I would'a joined the Navy. Jesus-H-Christ, you are old!" he continued, like a machine gun rattling off round after round.

"Joining this platoon to take advantage of these confused young men…" Now that was just an outright lie, Newman thought. "You ought to be ashamed of yourself, grandpa, these boys are just blossoming into the beautiful flowers they were always meant to be and along you come, the sugar daddy, bamboozling them into what I can only imagine are the most regrettable of man-on-man sessions!" But he had not had any "man-on-man sessions" yet, he wanted to scream. Again the sergeant was too quick for him.

"One question, Father Time," he asked. "Are you a bottom or a top?"

Newman took a slow, deep breath in a useless attempt to steady himself. "It did not happen to me," he said. His hands trembled and his eyes darted around the sergeant's face, scanning for even the slightest hint of compassion. "I saw what happened to them, but it did not happen to me!" he screamed. He had worked himself into a frenzy, and the sergeant's indifference terrified him. He felt himself take a step forward and he saw the sergeant's eyes widen at this brazen insubordination, but he couldn't stop himself. "Do you hear me? Do you hear me?" he shouted, "It did not happen to me!"

The sergeant marched a single step forward, to within an inch of Newman's face. "Soldier, you are gay until the United States military tells you otherwise."

Whatever courage Newman had mustered left him, and with it went the burning need to convince this sergeant of anything. Newman knew a dead end when he saw one.

"Ginger?" laughed the sergeant, catching Newman's name above his breast pocket.

"General Newman Ginger," he whispered.

"With a name like that it was only a matter of time, wasn't it soldier?"

"I'm telling you," muttered Newman, "I didn't inhale that gas."

"Now you're a faggot and a liar," growled the sergeant, his tone turning black. "Get back in line before I fuck you just to make a point."

Newman recoiled at the threat and stepped back into formation. It was as if the sergeant had not heard a single word Newman had said, as if he knew something that Newman didn't.

He began to doubt his own certainty. It would be one thing if a superior officer ignored Newman, they always did, but this lowly sergeant didn't even pause, didn't even stop to consider that Newman was anything other than a faggot. Was it official? Was it real? Was everyone else operating in some clear, distinct reality and Newman was the crazy one, stuck in some pathetic act of denial? He tried to imagine himself as a gay, and he envisioned a flaccid penis- the first test that came to mind- but it did nothing for him. He then imagined the penis slowly erecting itself. This was interesting, but not sexual. It was interesting in the way a two-headed horse would be interesting: you don't see that every day. It had been decades since Newman saw another man's penis, and he had succeeded in going a lifetime without seeing another man's erect penis. It wasn't until he envisioned the erect penis attached to a thrusting torso- the next level of his impromptu test- that Newman felt something. It wasn't much- a small surge of blood from his heart to his appendages- but it was enough. Newman felt a chill down his spine and a warm sensation in his crotch. He shook. Surely he was reacting to the thought of sexual movement in general. The thrusting motion, especially when carried out by any visually pleasing torso, would be enough to recall the act of intercourse, and that sense memory is what caused the rush. But he began to fill in the rest of the picture, to carry the test to its logical end. This torso, he discovered as the frame widened, belonged to his seventh grade English teacher, a young British import who Newman had adored. He had never seen the man naked, and never envisioned him naked until now, and he had absolutely no idea why the hell, of all the thrusting torsos and erect penises in the world, his mind was displaying Mr. Rooney's. But the thrusting continued as Mr. Rooney's chiseled arms and taut calves filled in, and finally, his face. Not perfectly handsome, Mr. Rooney was certainly attractive- symmetrical features, sincere eyes, and short hair. He was the man Newman saw himself becoming at 13, an age where his father was the last thing on earth he wanted to be, and here he was, naked as a dog, staring directly into Newman's eyes.

"Anyone need to touch up their makeup before we get started?" yelled the sergeant. "No? Good. Hit the course!"

The men sprinted toward the high wall thirty meters in front of them. It was safe to run now, most of them assumed, but a couple of the men shot wary looks toward the distant tree houses where the snipers could easily lean out and pick off a couple of them. If they were so inspired, or if word had not reached them that the new platoon was running the obstacle course, it could be a matter of a few seconds before the platoon was cut in half.

But no shots came, and no bodies hit the ground. In fact, the men moved so gracefully over the high wall, they stunned the sergeant and themselves. Chico pulled himself up the rope to the top of the wall and swung his legs over in a perfect half scissor, then let himself simply drop to the ground. He landed on both feet, had to squat to catch himself, but no one in the history of the high wall had leapt from the top without breaking something- an ankle, a wrist, in one unfortunate case, a neck. Chico, whose only athletic experience in life to this point had been a little pickup soccer and a pathetic display at boot camp, had nailed the landing, and had absolutely no idea how he had done so. He wasn't even sure he could do it again, so he sprinted away to the next station as quickly as possible, before anyone might ask him to repeat that gorgeous leap from a 22-foot high wall. Next was Richards, then James, Lincoln and Stirrups. All executed their climb and dismount with the grace and precision of Olympic gymnasts.

Deadweight was a different story. He could barely pull himself to the middle of the wall, even with the foot holes helpfully placed every eight or ten inches. He lowered himself back down and took a quick inventory of his vitals. All bad. His heart pounded, his chest tightened, he was dizzy, a little nauseous, and his arms and legs throbbed. It occurred to him that, even as the sergeant screamed and howled at him for being such a "fat lump of canned meat" and a "botched abortion" this was not boot camp, and he was under no obligation to finish anything. He was free to fail. He straightened up and hobbled around the wall. To the sergeant's chagrin, he was impotent to punish or prevent Deadweight or anyone else from quitting, on account of the scientist's need for untainted evidence- if the men chose to walk around the obstacle instead of participating in it, he needed to see that. So the most the sergeant could do was harangue, which he did with zeal. Newman didn't know any of this and opted to walk around the obstacles in silent, pouting protest. He shuffled past each in plain view of the sergeant and the two men who appeared to be evaluating the platoon's performance- a scientist, and a lumpy general whose uniform read "Burnam." When no reproach came, Newman pouted harder. At the monkey bars he deliberately walked between the sergeant and the bars, a move worth at least a good scream, if not a swift kick in the ass followed by pushups and some sort of cleaning duty. The sergeant let him pass without a word, and chose instead to harass the men who took the monkey bars seriously.

"Is that a Luger in your pocket, private, or are you just a giant fag for me?" he screamed at Lincoln. Lincoln was too distracted by his own skill to give the insult much weight. He whipped himself down the course, grabbing every other bar in long, smooth, swings, letting the momentum of the swing propel him through the air to every other bar. "I'm tempted to make some off-color remark about your natural ability on this particular obstacle, Private Two Strikes," he barked at James, "but the military has rather clear guidelines on hate speech! Besides, you queens bring out the gentleman in me!"

James ignored him, as did Chico, who walked across the top of the bars on his hands while his feet wiggled in the air for balance, which sent the sergeant into an apoplectic fit.

"You fancy fuck!" he screamed. "This isn't the god damn Ringling Brothers! Get your ass off my monkey bars!" Chico, however, had always wanted a talent and he was not about to stop, because he had no idea how he started. If he quit walking on his hands he had no idea if he would ever be able to do it again. This drove the sergeant even madder, and he hurled insult after insult at Chico, and everyone who followed. To the untrained eye he may have looked insane, screaming like a madman at small group of passersby who paid him no mind, becoming more enraged and verbose the less feedback he got, but to Deichmann he was exactly what the experiment needed, the control element, the lens through which to view this particular group's response to the same stimuli that confronts all soldiers at bootcamp.

When the men finally reached the firing range, the sergeant stopped screaming. It was the final stage in the battery of tests, and automatic gunfire tended to drown out the screams of even the most gifted tormenters. He pulled himself into a small watchtower about ten feet off the ground, directly behind the men. He was relieved to be elevated, away from this troop. They didn't fear him and it was disconcerting to put it mildly. In a few moments they would begin firing, a few grunts would swap the used targets out for new ones, they would fire some more, then everyone could call it a day.

The men, on the other hand, were excited and focused. To a man, they bore down on their sights, slowed their breathing and ripped their targets to shreds. James had never known military activity to be this much fun. He was used to making excuses for his lack of ability, which he assumed was borne of disinterest. Now it seemed he had it backwards. He was shocked by the joy of being good at something. Stirrups imagined the target was the sergeant at first, and then recalled a certain high school bully who beat him mercilessly for a solid two pubescent years and imagined his face on the target's black silhouette instead. Chico and Lincoln were also excellent shots suddenly, and enjoyed the feeling of handling the powerful AK-47. Deadweight loved the feel of being inside one of his video games. Though he hit the edges of the human shaped target in what would be the appendix and the shoulder, he reasoned he would at least cause the enemy serious discomfort and cumbersome medical expenses, which was good enough for now. Richards took each miss personally- he had shown exceptional grace and athleticism in the obstacles, and it was important to him to end the day's tests on a good note. He was raised to "finish strong," to end a challenge with the same courage and effort he showed at the beginning of the challenge, and this had served him well. He was a local sprinting champion in high school, unbeatable at the 100-meter and 400-meter dashes, and a good bit of that success was being able to ignore the pain of the lactic acid that fills a competitive athlete's muscles and cramps them into tight, throbbing pistons as they reach peak performance. Richards taught himself to finish strong by mentally blocking out the excruciating acid buildup until just after the race, allowing it to flood forward into his consciousness only after crossing the finish line. He suffered horrific cramps then, moments after the race when he would often collapse on the track. The cramps would ebb and flow over the course of an evening, waking him from a dead sleep as they spasmed into a knot half their original size, and he would wake up screaming. He suffered endless teasing from his brothers about these outbursts and the involuntary tears that would stream down his face as he begged and pleaded with his calves or hamstrings to untangle themselves. But he never changed. He knew the math: he won races because he ignored the consequences, and his brothers. The math was not nearly as clear when he applied it to the AK-47 and the target. The more he focused on hitting the center ring on the silhouette, the worse his aim. Each shot he bore down harder on the gun, squinted tighter and pulled the trigger with more deliberate speed, and each round hit a new ring out from the target's heart.

Newman, on the other hand, stood in the last alley, turned away from the target and faced the scientist and the general, pointed his gun to the sky, and pulled the trigger. The scientist and the general took note, of course, of the old man shooting his automatic weapon into the air for no reason. The scientist scribbled some notes while the general simply glared. Newman glared right back and fired into the sky until his clip was empty.

*

The metal legs of the bunk dragged across the linoleum floor and let out a horrific screeching sound. Newman could only move the heavy, two-story bed a couple feet at a time, and for the last fifteen minutes the men had been forced to listen to the intermittent screeches as he attempted to drag it from one end of the barrack into the bathroom at the opposite end.

"Why don't you just use one of the beds next to the bathroom?" shouted James.

"Who slept in it the last two nights?" Newman belted back. "I'm gonna catch whatever he's got? No, thanks. How about one of you boys get off your pretty ass, and..."

"How about you just admit you inhaled that gas like everyone else in here?" interrupted Stirrups.

Newman pretended not to hear him. Richards heard the entire exchange from the corner of the room, where he had been brooding in silence about his sad display on the firing range and the even more pathetic display from the defacto leader of the platoon, the old man, General Newman Ginger.

"Hey, old man," he said. Newman stopped dragging and stood up to catch his breath. "You see what we did out there?"

"I saw what you did," said Newman.

"What's that supposed to mean?"

"It appears you and I had about the same score on the range today, private," he said, grinning. "Only difference is, I wasn't aiming at the target."

Richards eased himself off the wall. "We were being watched today. They're trying to figure out what to do with us, and you sabotaged every test they put in front of us! You want to blow our careers? You want to blow your career?"

"I didn't sign up to babysit a bunch of queers," Newman shot back.

"We didn't sign up to become a bunch of queers," he said "but life's kinda funny like that."

"My heart breaks for you people, it really does."

"You people?" Richards crossed the room and the men jumped from their beds to try and intercept him, but he was too quick. Newman backpedaled as soon as he realized what was happening but his foot caught the leg of the bunk and he had to grab the mattress to avoid falling. That moment's hesitation was all the time Richards needed. He was on Newman in an instant, and punched him square in the broken nose, even used the bandage as a target, and sent the general sprawling across the ground.

"You self-loathing son of a bitch!" yelled Richards. The men pulled him away and Lincoln reluctantly helped Newman sit up and gain his bearings. Blood poured out of his already mangled nose and the make-shift bandage flapped around as Newman slowly rose to his feet. His head rattled and all he could hear was a high-pitched tone that felt like it was received from some other world, beamed directly into his brain in order to cripple him. He tried to open his eyes but the blood rushing to and from his nose forced them shut, and all he could do was cover them and sit helplessly on the bed until the blood clotted and the noise faded. He saw his wrinkled, pale hands as they reached for where his nose ought to be. He could make out a strapping young man standing between him and the angry mob, and clung to him. He had never felt so old.

Chapter 10

Deichmann watched Cadbury's eyes as they darted quickly across line after line of data, then down, then across, then down, then across. His eyes moved so fast, and he flipped to the next page so rapidly, either he was able to digest huge amounts of information with extreme alacrity, or he simply skimmed the flood of numbers, charts and conclusions looking for an easy answer, a hint, a bottom line.

Deichmann wiped tiny beads of sweat from his hairline without taking his eyes off Cadbury. He had laid out the unprecedented findings in such a way that any layman could see, with even a cursory glance...

"Speak, scientist," ordered Cadbury, as he tossed the spool-fed green and white ream onto a pile of reams that covered the desk and the floor.

"Mister Secretary, all empirical evidence points to a leap in physiological performance so dramatic..."

"Bigger, stronger, faster," interrupted Burnam.

"Better looking," said Fuller.

"The results are astounding," said Deichmann. "Not only did the olfactory manipulation fail to thwart the control population, it actually generated an entirely unrecognizable force of such superior talent…"

"What is this?" said Cadbury, and he aimed his laser pointer at the chart projected onto the wall of the War Room. "This flat line."

Deichmann whipped his head around to the chart, CONCLUSIONS ON PERFORMANCE ENHANCEMENTS AND DEGRADATIONS IN OLFACTORY CHEMICAL DIRECTIVE (OCD) TEST SUBJECTS (VOLUNTEER POPULATION ALL ACKNOWLEDGED WAIVER I-27C). The last part was insisted upon by the JAG's office, despite Deichmann's pleas. He felt it hampered the elegance of his conclusive chart and offered the secretary a constant reminder that he was free to dispose of the men as he wished. He was, however, thrilled that Cadbury had noticed the flat line. This was his ace in the hole.

"That flat line, sir, is the outlier," said Deichmann, his voice quivering.

"General Newman Ginger," scowled Fuller. "Claims he wasn't affected."

"All results support his conclusion," said Deichmann. "He is a resistant subject, someone whose biological makeup is unaffected by this powerful chemical directive."

"Denial," muttered Cadbury.

"Fifty, single, very, very handsome," said Fuller. "All signs point to gay."

"But his test results are so astonishingly inferior," said Deichmann. "It's overwhelmingly possible that he is, in fact, straight. For that reason alone…"

"Overwhelmingly possible?" said Cadbury. A sliver of hope rose in Deichmann.

"In for a penny, in for a pound is what I always say," said Fuller.

Cadbury considered this, then nodded. "In for a penny, in for a pound."

Deichmann sank. He had banked on Cadbury's desire to save the straight in the group as a given. He had underestimated the man's fear. In thinking about the secretary's accomplishments in battle as a young man, in politics as a middle-aged man, in leadership as an old man he had forgotten that Cadbury was, through it all, just a man. What was known was easy. What was new was not. He would have to switch tactics, to adjust and improvise, "A&I" in military parlance. He knew the only force greater than fear is self-interest, and what could interest Cadbury more than superior military talent?

Cadbury kicked a stack of printouts from under his feet and stood to leave.

"Sir!" screamed Deichmann. "With one exception, we are looking at unparalleled talent!"

"Suppose it spreads," said Cadbury. "Suppose they multiply. If I read this correctly, we could be looking at the greatest fighting force the world has ever known."

"Yes! Exactly!"

"Well, clearly they must be destroyed."

Deichmann couldn't believe his ears. "Sir, the talents of these men, if harnessed…"

"Could take down an army twice their size, including ours!"

"They are ours!" pleaded Deichmann.

Fuller stood to leave as well. "Sir, how do we disappear this platoon without generating more questions?"

"Disappear them?" screamed Deichmann. "Have you seen their test scores? We should turn the entire Army gay!"

"Like the Spartans," said Burnam, who was determined to appear involved, despite his exhaustion.

"They could conquer the world!" said Deichmann.

"Including us," said Cadbury. "If they turned?"

"They could colonize us, Deichmann," said Fuller. "Enslave us. Force us to perpetrate disgusting, amoral acts upon one another."

"There is a bunker in northern Iraq," said Cadbury. "The last remnant of Iraq's occupation of the Kurdish north." He spoke directly to Fuller. Deichmann knew it was over. He had fought and lost. The platoon, his experiment, the future of sexuality-enhanced conflict was all going to be washed down the drain, erased from memory, erased from history. It would be done with the artful simplicity of most disappearances, made to look like casualties of war, an assignment gone wrong. "It's a training ground for a few hundred of Saddam's elite Mukhabarat," continued Cadbury. "They guard the fort like Allah himself was inside. Send our boys to… investigate. Tell them it's a rescue mission or something. They won't be back. But just to be safe, put General…" His voice trailed off. He snapped his fingers and searched for the name.

"General Newman Ginger," smiled Fuller.

"Yes," said Cadbury. "Put General Newman Ginger in charge."

"You can't do that!" exploded Deichmann, standing.

"Pardon?" said Cadbury, his fury barely contained.

"You can't send them to that fortress! It's a suicide mission!"

"The Godless scientist wants to be the conscience of the group," laughed Cadbury. "How quaint. We let you out of your cage and you make this mess, and you dare to challenge how I clean it up?" Cadbury moved toward him. "Now, you go back to your Bunsen burners, and your adorable little theories, Doctor, and leave the security of this great nation to men who aren't afraid to get their hands a little dirty, before we disappear you, too."

Deichmann collapsed into his chair as Cadbury marched out, followed by Fuller. So it was written, and so it shall be, he heard himself say. So it shall be.

*

Newman sat on an overturned milk crate he found behind the barracks and licked his ice cream sandwich. They had surprised the men with a hot meal and a small cooler with ice cream sandwiches, and Newman had grabbed his and darted outside immediately, always keeping a stiff spine, but thrilled to escape the awkward glances and forced politeness of the platoon. A white handkerchief dangled from his nose, thick with dried blood at the top where it was jammed in to prevent leakage. The bandaid stretched across his nose had small brown and purple blots and seemed to serve no real purpose beyond aesthetics. Newman felt it would remind people to be careful around his nose. Richards and the men, on the other hand, agreed it would make an excellent bullseye should the old man act up again.

Across the barracks, through the chain link fence that surrounded barrack 175, he could see shirtless soldiers playing a spirited game of volleyball, replete with spikes and dives, cheers and high-fives. After a particularly impressive spike, two sweaty teammates hugged. The setter took a short break to pour water on his head and down his back and chest. Newman found the slow pace of the sport boring; he hated to watch the ball arc back and forth, back and forth, only to be thumped up into the air again for another round of back and forth, back and forth. It was especially tiresome to watch these boys play, for they had little skill. They seemed to enjoy the company, the camaraderie, the ass-slapping jolliness of the event mixed with the occasional physicality of slamming oneself to the ground. Though they were having a grand time, there was little payoff for the spectator, thought Newman.

His eyes drifted to the outdoor weight lifting arena where more shirtless soldiers performed dead-lifts, squat-thrusts, latissimus pulls and bicep curls. Their rippling muscles seemed to explode to twice their size when contracted. In the bright mid-day sunlight they looked like small titans to Newman. They lifted and pressed and pulled with such intensity it felt to Newman like they were perfectly unaware of the rest of the world. This was certainly a byproduct of age, he knew, but he had long ago begun to relish physical training as a time to reflect. It was in this quiet space and time, running on the small, damp roads that wove through and around his town that he came to understand himself and his decision-making process, why he had spoken to a colleague in a certain way, how he would approach this superior to make that request. Exercise had shifted from physicality to work therapy. And now, as he watched these men who seemed to believe there was no achievement greater than the next repetition, he felt both the distant condescension of a parent and the pride of a grandparent. They'll learn, he thought. Someday, they'll learn. But for the moment, he thought, he was proud to be in the same army as these miniature titans.

He took another bite of his ice cream sandwich and let his gaze drift to his men. It was truly staggering how quickly their bodies had transformed. As they threaded the barbed wire atop the fence in teams of two, he watched their once lumpy, sagging torsos tighten and twist. He could identify tightly-wound muscle groups on these men where just a few short days ago elusive, unidentifiable swaths of skin and fat bulges covered huge stretches of body. He felt his nose throb and took a long lick of his ice cream sandwich.

*

"I don't know how to put this, Richards," whispered Deadweight. "But I feel… funny." He looked to Richards for some flash of recognition.

"Hell, Dwight, I understand," said Richards, focused on threading the barbed wire over then under its steel string guide wire. The thick leather gloves made every loop difficult, the speed of the entire process was akin to counting blades of grass, but the men, following Richards' example, never complained.

"You feel it, too?" said Deadweight.

"Sure I do. Being… gay," he could barely say it. "It's new to all of us. We're all a little… spooked." He wasn't getting it, Deadweight knew.

"No, Richards, it's something else."

"Dwight, get back here and hold this pole," giggled Stirrups as he struggled to secure a loose fence post. Lincoln punched him in the arm and together they jammed the pole deeper into the ground. Though some of the men attempted to make the best of this terrifying, bizarre situation, Dwight "Deadweight" Butterman struggled to do so. Each night since the experiment fever dreams plagued his sleep. He was a butcher, a mailman, a symphony conductor, a rapist, a high school principal, a child, a grandparent and he always wanted one thing: food. Night after night he watched himself gorge on raw meat, deli sandwiches, turkey legs, human flesh in a handful of dreams, pizza, pasta, ice cream, potatoes, mashed potatoes, and when he tried to stop eating, every remaining ounce would be scooped up and forced down his throat by family and friends. They had different faces but he recognized them all the same. No matter how much he thrashed and railed against them and cried out each night, the attacks would continue. Each night he became a grotesque, bloated, swollen mass of sweaty, pale fat. Each night hair sprouted in itchy clumps on his face and hands and lower back and became caked with the dripping fat of the bounty being shoved down his throat, as his screams were muffled by biscuits and ham and the hands of his loved ones. He would die under the weight of their forced feedings, nightly, feeling the tightening of a noose in his chest that slowly, methodically encircled his heart and arteries, as his bloated, clumsy arms swung helplessly into the air to reach for the hangman who was not there. Even his eyes glazed over, coated with the gelatinous residue of a thousand meals and just as the last breath wheezed out of his lungs, he would awaken.

He spent the first hours of each day analyzing the nuances of those bits he could remember, attempting to rationalize the most frightening parts. By the time he felt composed enough to interact with the platoon he was so shamed at his own hunger he wouldn't eat. He stared at his meals as if confused by their lack of aggression, as if waiting for them to spring from the plate into his mouth or nostrils as they had the night before. He distrusted his food. Hunger was replaced more and more each day with curiosity. The less he ate, the more he noticed the world around him. He smelled new scents, like the concrete floor of the barracks and the clean sheets of the mostly unused beds. The exhaustion made it impossible to enjoy the new scents, and the terror of another night's sleep encroaching made it difficult to remember them, but each day he took what small comfort he could.

"General?" called Richards. "Hey, Ginger? You gonna give us a hand, or you gonna sit there and suck on that treat?"

"Fuck you, private," called Newman, as he took another lick.

"You coming onto me, general?"

Newman shot up from his milk crate to scream at the kid but stood too quickly and became dizzy as the blood swirled around his head. He heard a vehicle approaching, and when he opened his eyes again, General Fuller sat in a small gator truck in front of him, chauffeured by some young pleeb, no doubt new to the base and thrilled to have such a prestigious assignment. The pleeb jumped from the gator, stuck a key into the lock of the fence gate, and opened it for Newman.

"Get in, Ginger," ordered Fuller.

Newman was wary of his old colleague given the treatment he and the platoon had suffered these last few days. Still, he popped the last bite of his ice cream sandwich into his mouth, brushed his hands off along the front of his shirt, and shuffled around to the rear of the gator. As the truck peeled away, the last thing he saw was the tiny platoon, barbed wire in hand, building their own prison. He felt a tinge of sadness for them. The poor bastards have no idea, he thought.

*

"Have you been eating? Are they feeding you okay?" asked Fuller, with whatever signs of concern he could muster. The windowless room under the mess hall was drab enough, he thought. If he were going to get this old battle-ax to go along he would need to brighten up his approach, massage him a bit.

"Yes, yes, absolutely," said Newman.

"And the other boys? Are they… behaving?"

"Yes, of course, they're a good lot."

"Good, good." said Fuller. "No hard feelings about leaving you in there with those, uh…"

"Of course, no, none at all."

"You understand, of course…"

"Absolutely, yes."

"You understand, of course, why it had to happen that way?"

"Sure. Certainly," said Newman. "Special treatment for me and all of a sudden you've got a mutiny on your hands." Newman's eyes shifted around the room as he looked for someone to open the door through which he could exit for good, and return to his life.

"Exactly, Newman. That's exactly right." Fuller's eyes remained fixed on Newman. He studied the man for any sign of outrage, for a show of strength, of fury, of disgust. Though Newman's fate was sealed, Fuller held onto some small hope that his old colleague stood even a slight chance of dying with dignity over there.

"So how do we extricate me, now, without causing..."

"First, let me say how much I admire your staunch heterosexuality, Ginger."

"Yes, thank you. How do we extricate me, then, without..."

"I know it must be a challenge to remain faithful to your principles in such an environment."

"Not really."

"Hmm."

"What?"

"Newman, we go back a long ways."

"You believe me, don't you, Sidney? You came to my wedding."

"And testified in your divorce."

"What's that supposed to mean?"

Fuller sat back in his chair and stared at Newman. In the army, there are rules. There are protocols and procedures. A man knows when he's fouled, and a single look from a superior can send him reeling through the codes of conduct- written and unwritten- with such clarity and speed he can usually assign his own punishment. Newman was suddenly embarrassed to have entered this interrogation room with any hope. As far as the army was concerned, he should have known, he was out. They didn't have to ask, he didn't have to tell. They saw him, in grainy black and white, inhale the very same gas those other poor bastards inhaled, and his fate was sealed, days ago, irrevocably.

"You said this was my chance, Sydney."

"It was, Newman. It was exactly that. You spun the wheel. Sometimes she lands on red. Sometimes she lands on black."

Newman felt his chest tighten. He had always had his post to cling to, his career in the army, his steady paycheck, some outside station that validated his existence and shielded him from the vagaries of chance. Without his post, what did he have? Only his house, a ghost shell that served only to occupy his time during the darkest hours of the night, when he was not allowed at his post. From the moment he left the court martial he had believed, deep in the darkest corners of his mind where he still allowed unreasonable hope to loiter, he would someday return to his post. But now, in this moment, he knew the small voice of unreasonable hope must be silenced. He was finished.

"You're not sending me back with those men, Sydney!" he cried. "If I'm gay, fine, discharge me. I know the rules. I like men. I'm a first class faggot, General Fuller. You've caught me. I'll take my walking papers and be on my way, but I am not going back to that barracks to be locked away like some kind of monster!"

"Not so fast, Ginger," said Fuller. Fuller gave a slight gesture with his hand toward the two-way mirror facing both men and a new pleeb rushed into the room with a pitcher of water and a small plastic cup. Newman felt his face flush as he imagined the pleeb- some snot-nosed kid without a single scalp on his belt-watching him squirm and plead for his freedom, and fail. "Drink up, Newman."

Newman did as he was told. He could feel the pitcher ground him to reality, to a faucet, to a kitchen somewhere on the barracks, filled with soldiers who would leave for wars, who would experience unwritten futures in far away lands. It was his first taste of the world outside his own since the court martial and the water was crisp and cool, a gift from some benevolent stranger who Newman could never properly thank.

"Back at the Pentagon, we saw the test scores, and those boys are off the map."

"I tanked every one of those tests!"

"You personally, you played the game by your own rules, and that makes you uniquely qualified to be a leader of men," said Fuller. "I want to present you with an opportunity, Newman." Newman's hand shook as he poured another cupful of ice water. "I know how badly you want a mission…"

"Now that you think I'm some queer, now you want me back in the field?" he asked, eyeing Fuller suspiciously.

Fuller slid a thin dossier across the table to Newman and opened it. Inside was a single sheet of crisp, white paper with thick, even, black print, and a red CLASSIFIED stamp across it all. The stamp was so new it had smudged when the dossier was closed on top of it. "Twelve of our Seals are holed up in a Mukhabarat compound deep in the Turkish north of Iraq.

God only knows what those camel-fuckers are doing to them as we speak."

Newman was lost. He had been reviled by his army only a week ago, and that was before going gay. But the offer was so ripe, so sweet, the oddity of its timing and origin barely registered. A rescue mission. A chance to save the lives of elite forces. It was troublesome that a dozen Navy Seals had been overtaken by these Mukhabarat, and Newman was being sent with six recently-former vegetables to rescue them. But, he thought, the boys had been growing into themselves lately, beefing up. And was it not a vote of confidence in his leadership abilities, that they would ask him, General Newman Ginger to lead this mission? After all, they wouldn't offer him the mission unless they believed he could succeed where others had failed. But what was it that gave them such confidence, he would like to know? He would very much like to know. But he wasn't about to ask Fuller. He wasn't about to reveal the crippling doubt that thumped through his brain at that very moment. They would strip him of the mission and lump him back in with the fags, and then who knows what fate would befall him. Without a leader, without a true General, would there even be a mission? And if not, what then? No, this was the moment. This was his chance to break out of his caste, a last best chance, and he knew it. General Newman Ginger had just been handed his very own platoon, for the first time since The Shit.

*

"This is ridiculous, Ginger," yelled Stirrups. "We've sacrificed enough already."

The resistance surprised Newman. Perhaps it was his approach, he thought. He walked into the platoon's New Years Eve celebration just as the clock struck midnight, kicked off the tiny radio Lincoln discovered on the long walk from the firing range back to barracks the day before, and launched into his call to action right there, on the spot. Yes, perhaps he should have waited until morning, allowed the men an evening's sleep and all the hope and cheer that comes with a new day and a new year, and in this case, a new millennium, before hitting them with the news they would be risking their newly upturned lives on a rescue mission in one of the most distant, dangerous corners of the earth. Next time, he thought, he would wait until morning.

"I don't think you understand," said Newman. "The boys upstairs are willing to ignore your new… preference, lets' say, in order to give you this unbelievable opportunity."

"Preference?" shouted Stirrups. "You think I prefer this to who I've been for the last twenty two years?"

"What's all this 'you guys' and 'you boys' shit," said Cruz. "You got gassed, too."

Stirrups laughed. "It didn't happen to me!" he mocked. "It didn't happen to me!" The men laughed. Newman could feel the meeting slipping away from him. Stirrups was on a roll. "I think it did happen to him," purred Stirrups. "I see the way you look at me, Ginger." He looked directly into Newman's eyes. The men played along, and turned their heads all at once to await Newman's reaction.

"That's scurrilous!" screamed Newman. "That's baseless!"

"What do you want from us, Ginger?" called Richards, from the back of the group. "You got a big speech planned about how we should all be thrilled to go serve, to go make another sacrifice for Uncle Sam?"

"I'm just telling you how it's gotta be."

"We gotta go?" asked Richards.

Newman held up the thin dossier from Fuller. "We got a team of special ops help prisoner down in that valley. They're sending us, for Christ's sake, to go rescue them. You want to turn your back on these boys?"

"No, the military never turns its back on its own, right?" said Richards. He glared at Newman.

"Alright, so you leave here," began Newman. He had prepared for this, for the backlash from a small group of overworked men who wanted nothing more than to get home. He knew this scenario well. This was war. This was Vietnam, but it was also Korea, and Normandy, and Sparta, and Waterloo. This was a general and his men, on the precipice. What lay beyond, well, that was unwritten. He silently worked through the angles on the long, lonely ride from his meeting with Fuller back to 175. He came up with nothing. There was no angle, no balm, no salve. They were stepping into a shitstorm, and the only thing worse would be sticking around here- Fuller declined to answer the question of what would happen to defectors, to those who passed on the mission, and Newman didn't press. He could read between the lines.

He decided to lay it on the line for his boys, to speak the truth and have faith in them to make the right decision once they'd heard all the facts. If that didn't work, well...

"Then what?" he asked. "You go back to your desk jobs? Back to serving slop in the mess, or pushing papers around the back office? I don't think so, boys. It's all on videotape. We're gone. Every one of us. So we have this opportunity, here. We can accept failure, and defeat, and dishonorable discharge. Or, we can return to the world victorious, as heroes who saved the lives of brothers we've never met. When you return home, who do you want to be?"

Chapter 11

Deadweight tugged on the tether that connected him to the plane's jump rack. It looked like a leash, he thought, he was being dragged like a dog halfway around the world for this mission. Luckily he was sweating still less these days, and was more comfortable in the sweat that did pour out, as if it was something to be embraced for a job well done and not something to be feared as a destroyer of cotton underpants. Just this morning he had broken into a significant sweat when he stuffed his pack with a handful of clothes and MRE's, and carried to it to the waiting transport, which was a sweatbox itself. But by the time the transport clamored onto the highway he was quite comfortable, and he found himself having to search for the anxiety within. All the ingredients were there- he was clammy, he had just exerted himself, he was in a moving vehicle- but for some reason, they refused to coalesce into the explosive material that combusted into sweat, his life-long companion. In its place, there was only a buzzing.

Some distant hum called him forward into the next minute, and the next.

"Stirrups," he said. "I feel weird."

"That's why it's called queer, buddy."

Deadweight shook his head. No one listened to him. It wasn't their fault, he knew, he just wasn't the type that people listened to. He was more the type people purposefully avoided, for fear he would sweat on them, or complain to them, or depress them with his appearance. He slunk back into his seat and listened to the gentle buzz inside, this new, persistent companion that insisted he keep looking to the future and not the inglorious now.

Though Stirrups had taken on his new flamboyant persona with relish, he turned it down a notch with Deadweight. He saw the chubby, morose boy as a younger-brother, weak and fearful in the face of the big, scary world, hiding behind his older brother's legs and only peeking out when things were quiet. It reminded Stirrups of himself at thirteen. The bullies gleefully hunted down the weakest on the playground, reenacting some emotional torture they had undergone at home on the scrawniest, most timid boys who dared show themselves at recess. While most boys were bursting into men with eruptions of height and acne and anger, and traveling in packs to leer at the girls who were erupting in fits of height and acne and gossip, young Terry Stryker watched from the sidelines, hoping his thin legs and petit frame would help him blend into the background. Bullies, however, seemed to have an extraordinary gift for finding the boys who tried the hardest to hide, Terry included. Had it not been for the size and demeanor of his older brother, he would have received the severe, merciless beatings that his friends received on a weekly basis, which he often witnessed in horror from behind his brother's legs. The beatings seemed to curtail in the winters, however, because both predators and prey huddled indoors, and it was during this uneasy truce that Terry reflected most on who he would like to become, should he survive to adulthood. He committed to protect the weak, as his brother had done for him, to become an older brother to someone, or to an entire country, and that led him to the army. The army, however, found him about as useful as those bullies found him, and so he was here, on this plane, and grateful to have Deadweight hiding behind his legs.

"You ever jumped before?" asked Cruz. He had to shout to be heard. The V-22 Osprey was stripped of all the sound-reducing conveniences of modern airplanes, it was a flying tin can, an airborne school bus with a gaping jump-hole where a door should be. Between the wind and the turbulent rattle of metal parts flying through space at 300 miles per hour, scarcely a word could be heard without screaming.

The men looked from one to another. In the rush to pack it hadn't occurred to the platoon that they would each be jumping solo out of a plane. They had focused more on the landing-in-hostile-territory aspect of the plan. They had all just sort of assumed that someone would show them how to get from the plane to the hostile territory, and had devoted all their terror to the endless possibilities of what awaited them on the ground.

Richards stood and pulled himself along the hand-grips leading to the front of the plane, where Newman stood tightening the straps of his pack. "I think you should say something to the men, Newman."

"That's 'General Ginger' to you now" he said.

"You prefer 'General *Ginger*' to 'Newman?'" said Richards, genuinely surprised. Before Newman could scold him for talking back, the co-pilot appeared.

"Mercenaries have heavily fortified this area," he shouted over the rattle of the plane. "But don't worry. The vast majority of jumpers make it to the ground, just like this." He covered his crotch with his left hand and pinned his helmet to his head with his right. Newman suddenly felt nauseous.

"Jump point, thirty seconds," yelled the co-pilot.

Newman turned to the men and pulled a crumpled sheet of paper from his helmet. He had prepared a brief statement for this moment.

"As we prepare to jump into heavily-fortified enemy territory, I'm sure you have a lot on your minds," he said. "I just want you to know, I've given this some serious thought, and I've decided to put aside any disinclinations I may have about your sexual orientation, at least for now. For the sake of the mission at hand, I would like to improve morale by announcing that I'm going to pretend each of you is straight like me, and not…" His voice trailed off. He stuffed the paper back into his helmet. "Well, you know."

Stirrups made a mock, half-assed "Hoo-ah" yell, but didn't get the laugh he was looking for. On top of fear, the men were weighted down with the misery of having to follow General Newman Ginger into one of the most dangerous theaters in all the world.

"Jump point!" yelled the co-pilot. "Go, go, go!"

"Jump point!" echoed Newman. "Gentlemen," he called. "Once more, unto the breach!" He covered his crotch and pinned his helmet to his head and leapt from the plane. Each of the men followed silently. A few seconds and a few hundred feet later the platoon formed a circle, linked hands and fell together. They had slipped into this formation without a word, without a gesture. It was somehow immediately, thoughtlessly, second nature. After a moment's time, they split in half and formed two circles- Deadweight, Richards and Stirrups formed one spinning circle, and Cruz, Lincoln and James formed the second- then split again, into three pairs. As they fell they spun like wagon wheels clamoring forward in time against a dead black backdrop. They split again, each man pulling away from his partner, falling on his own into the abyss. Somehow they had known how to fall, how to slide into form, how to survive, and each pulled the cord, released the tension in their core and let their legs whip downward as their shoulders shot upward, and without a single thought, each man drifted now smoothly toward the sand below.

Somewhere nearby, Newman plummeted alone toward the unforgiving earth. He pulled his cord, the chute snapped into place, whipped his shoulders up and legs down, and reduced his velocity from terminal to manageable. When he caught his breath, he realized he was alone. He tried to look up but the chute blocked his view almost entirely and he could see nothing in the night sky around him.

Newman saw the sand rushing up at his legs, and he tried to swing them forward, to catch his heels and give him a chance at a running start. The wind resistance was too great and he only managed to tangle them before they crumpled beneath him. The chute collapsed onto him as he toppled face-first into the sand. Stunned and woozy, he ran through his major joints and muscles, and neck and back, and was relieved he could feel and wiggle everything. He was suddenly exhausted as the adrenaline subsided and he was left with only the pounding of his heart and a high-pitched squeal in his ears, like the sound of a dentist's drill amplified to deafening levels. If he closed his eyes, he thought, it would all go away. He could sleep for days. A better opportunity to check out would never present itself. He could disappear under this soft nylon blanket forever. Under here, he could see nothing, feel nothing. He was hidden from the world, and the wind-whipped sand would surely cover him in a matter of hours. He could drift away silently and peacefully without shame, and his children would only know he died in service to country, 'in battle.' It was perfect, in a way. Yes, perhaps he should just close his eyes for a bit, he thought.

He heard the first thud a few meters away. The boys were landing. He was awake now, fully. He had been given a mission, and if his boys made it down alive they would need their leader. With the same alacrity with which he was willing to die he was again ready to lead. He brushed it off as if he had only been considering a brief nap, a respite, and forgot almost immediately about the darkest feelings that had overtaken him only moments before. He did not want to wait for one of his boys to land and help him untangle the chute, a two-man job. He must show them he was master of his own fitness, he thought. He pulled his combat blade from his hip and began cutting through the nylon and as he chopped his way out, he saw Stirrups slip from the air into a dead sprint, and slowly bring himself to a halt as his chute fell neatly behind him. Then Deadweight, then Lincoln and Cruz all glided onto terra firma with the same grace, and Newman cut faster.

"Where the hell is this village?" asked Stirrups.

Newman had cut himself free and stumbled over to the group, still woozy. "Boys, I'm sure we're close. Private Two Strikes, our location, please?"

Brooklyn pulled the GPS communication system from his pack and feverishly entered the ten-digit security code. He studied the device, then looked to the group.

"Well?" asked Newman. "How far are we from our contact point?"

"One or two…" James's voice trailed off. "Countries," he finished.

"What?" asked Newman.

"We're in Lebanon," he said.

"They dropped us in fucking Lebanon?" cried Stirrups.

"Don't get hysterical," said Newman. "I'm sure there's a perfectly good…" Newman was interrupted by the unmistakable rumble of a second V-22 Osprey. Thank god, he thought, they consulted their global positioning system, discovered their error, and…

The men looked to the sky as the rumble approached and then disappeared. Crestfallen, they looked to one another for some sort of explanation.

There was a loud crash in the distance, wood-on-wood, a heap of lumber crashing to earth. Then another, and another. Newman led the stunned platoon toward the sound of the first crash, and with flashlights drawn, they came upon a large wooden crate, a parachute collapsed haphazardly behind it and draped over one side.

"Ah!" said Newman. "A little good luck present from the brass."

"What is it?" asked Richards.

"It's a surprise," said Stirrups, dryly. He had begun to doubt the military's commitment to this mission, starting with their seeming indifference to having dropped the platoon 500 miles and two hostile nations away from their target.

"I love surprises," said Lincoln, oblivious to Stirrups' sarcasm.

Without a word, Deadweight sprinted through the platoon toward the ten-foot tall wooden crate, and leapt. He jackknifed his right knee into the air to propel him upward, arms outstretched to the heavens. His right foot stuck to the top of the crate, his left leg slammed into the side with a dull thud, and he grabbed the lip of the wood, and pushed himself the rest of the way up onto the roof of the crate. The platoon stood dumbfounded. It hadn't been graceful, but Deadweight just jumped ten feet into the air, from sand. And stranger, he hadn't seemed to notice. He whipped the industrial flashlight from his belt and began hammering at the cracked joints of the crate.

The men built a perimeter of flashlights by jamming them into the sand and aiming them at Deadweight and the front of the crate. Richards and Cruz jammed their flashlights into the crack that slowly formed between the roof and the front panel of the crate, and worked them as levers to pry the panel loose. The rest of the platoon grabbed it and pulled as the men with flashlights wedged further and further. Newman stood aside. When Lincoln first reached his hand into the crate to pull on the forward wall, Newman called out, "Get your hand in there, Lincoln, reach right in!" When the men joined in and began to tug on the forward wall in unison with the flashlight team, he called out, "Give it a good tug! All together now!" The men, for their part, ignored him or couldn't hear him over the pulsing groan of bent wood and the screech of nails as they slid out of the side walls of the crate.

"On three!" shouted Richards. The forward wall was half-open, but one good tug from six men would topple it. "One, two, three!" The men all pulled at once and the wall collapsed, and hunks of twisted metal spilled into the sand.

Newman picked up the near end of a large, curved piece of steel and studied it.

"What the hell is that?" asked Stirrups.

"That's a MasterFlow," said Cruz. "Stainless steel." The platoon members all stared at him with the same clueless expression. "It's a muffler."

"There's a note!" said Richards, and he pulled a small white envelope from the scrap heap and ripped it open.

Newman dropped the muffler and snatched the note from Richards. "Dearest Fighting 175th," he read aloud. "May the good Lord watch over you on this long, hard journey, and provide you the strength and courage to, temporarily, at least, abate eroticism."

The men looked to one another for some sign of how to interpret the cryptic note, but each was as puzzled as the other. "Signed, Secretary William Cadbury."

Richards sniffed the pink envelope. "Eternity," he observed.

"Private Two Strikes!" exclaimed Newman. The platoon whipped around to see a fully assembled chassis- frame and suspension, supported by four wide tires, and the beginnings of a steering column.

"I don't know what happened," said Brooklyn. "All of a sudden it just clicked."

"Were you a mechanic?" asked Richards.

"I used to work at a gas station. I pumped gas, changed fluids…"

"I understand," said Deadweight, as he climbed down from the crate. "Ever since it happened, it's like I'm me, I'm still me… only more."

"Hogwash," said Newman. "It's all in your head, soldier!"

"You saw Deadweight's leap with your own eyes," said Richards.

"And how do you explain this?" said Stirrups, as he inspected the chassis.

"What's gonna happen to the rest of us?" asked Cruz.

"You don't believe this garbage do you?" said Newman. "The crate is regulation. It looks tall, but with a good wind at my back, I'm sure I could… And the chassis? It's just a few hunks of metal! A couple wheels, a frame, a steering column, a couple axels," he panted. "If I was his age I could lug those parts over, and, and, and lump them together in a couple minutes, I'm sure of it!" The men looked at the ground, or at each other. "Nothing is happening. Look at me. I'm still just plain old me!"

"But you didn't inhale that gas," said Richards.

"Are we all going to change?" said Lincoln.

"What am I going to become?" said Cruz.

"What were you before?" said Richards.

"I worked in a deli. I made sandwiches."

"I was going to law school," said Lincoln.

"I was gonna be an English teacher," said Stirrups.

"Pizza delivery," said Deadweight.

"I was just a soldier," said Richards. All eyes turned to Newman. The platoon's belief in their rapid evolution had weakened his resolve to prove the opposite. He would not break, he thought, but he would bend now, for expediency. Besides, the longer they stood here like sitting ducks, the more attention they would call to themselves, he thought, even in the middle of the Lebanese desert. Yes, he was only going to participate for expediency, he reminded himself.

"I was just a general," he said.

*

Brooklyn balled up his undershirt, now ruined with grease, and used it to wipe the sweat off his chest and neck. He stood panting with the rest of the platoon, all in various states of undress, covered in grease and sweat. In front of them sat a fully assembled, neon pink humvee.

"Job well done boys," offered Richards. He weighed the insult against the ease of travel and decided simply to be grateful they weren't expected to walk to Iraq.

"Have you lost your senses," said Newman, who had watched the build with disgust. "I am not riding in that monstrosity. I am a heterosexual male, and I will not be treated like some two-dollar queer! I will not stand for it!" The platoon had made the same bargain that Richards had, to ignore the heinous and demeaning joke, to let it slip into the dark desert night as if it never existed, and instead cling to the practicality of it, the benefit of four wheels over no wheels. But with every word Newman brought it back into the light. He dug his toe into the sand and dragged it ten feet, making a line between the men and the new pink humvee. "This is where I draw the line! The line has been drawn! As your commanding officer, I order you to…"

Richards stepped over the line to stand next to the vehicle. "Two-dollar queers over here."

Stirrups strode over the line and spun to face Newman. "This charade has gone on long enough, pops."

"Well, I built the god damn thing," said Two Strikes, "I'm sure as shit gonna ride in it."

"I ain't walking," said Cruz as he crossed the line.

"Me either," muttered Deadweight, who stepped directly on the line, to add insult to injury. Only Lincoln remained.

"Lincoln?" asked Richards.

"He's the commanding officer," said Lincoln, to one in particular, even as he took a step toward the line.

"Have you no pride, young man?" asked Newman.

"We have a mission to complete, Lincoln," said Richards. He didn't have to push harder. Lincoln crossed the line without another thought.

"I'm sorry, General," he said.

"Well, I for one have some dignity left," said Newman. "Even one ounce is enough to prevent me from stepping into that giant bubble-gum colored fuck-you to warfare!"

"Dignity won't get you to Kirkuk, General," said Richards. With that, he and the platoon filed silently into the humvee.

Chapter 12

"According to the GPS," said Brooklyn, "the Syrian border is just ahead." The men stiffened. They had traveled 100 miles through the Lebanese desert under cover of night, but the black sky now began to reveal hints of blue and grey. They would enter Syria in a giant pink bullseye just as daylight broke. Brooklyn took some comfort in the thobes they had all donned, as part of their cover. They correctly assumed their American military fatigues would cause great consternation in this part of the world, and had sewn seven hastily-crafted ankle-length coveralls from their bedsheets and pillow cases before departing the barracks, despite the protestations of one aging general, who felt it was un-American and demeaning to "wear a dress" while on officially duty.

Stirrups had been unusually quiet, but not from exhaustion. There was a certain pinch to this joke, a sharpness to it, a distinct ugliness in the gift of the pink humvee. "I tell you babes, I'm gonna burn this goddamn car to the ground," he said to anyone in earshot, "I simply can not be the killing machine I was born to be inside this thing, I just can't." The men cracked up, they were desperate for a joke and Stirrups was grateful he could both vent and provide a little levity.

Newman rode shotgun and pretended to flip through the brief on the compound in which the SpecOps were held prisoner. In truth, he could not read in the car because it upset his stomach, but the men refused to let him drive and he wanted to look busy. He flipped page after page, and when he reached the end, he started again. Richards pretended not to notice as he drove through the desert and into the rolling mountains along the border. He felt sorry for the old man, and wanted to spare him further embarrassment if at all possible, though the son of a bitch did not make it easy.

The humvee crested a small, rocky gap and the border crossing came into view. Three armed guards stood and positioned themselves in front of the fortified gate. As the humvee approached, the guards rose their Russian-made AK47's and yelled in Arabic for the vehicle to halt. Newman pulled the pistol from his hip, careful to keep it below the dash, and cocked it, to ensure when the shit hit the fan, he would have at least one round in the chamber. "Alright, boys," he whispered, "the moment of truth."

"Screw that," sniped Stirrups, as he leapt out of the backseat and marched toward the guards.

"Stirrups!" called Richards.

"Stand down!" screamed Newman. "Stryker!" He tried to unbuckle his seatbelt but it was stuck. He tugged and thrashed but the belt only tightened. The guards screamed in Arabic and waved their AK47's frantically. To the platoon's surprise, Stirrups screamed back in what seemed to be Arabic as well. Suddenly the guards swung their guns to the humvee. The men ducked and shuffled in the vehicle, Two Strikes tried to load his weapon but dropped the clip under the seat. Richards turned around to yell at the men to keep calm while Newman loudly cursed the day the seatbelt was invented. Stirrups screamed louder at the guards, who swung their guns back to him. The platoon pushed each other toward the humvee's doors, but the child locks pinned them in. The men screamed at Richards to let them out. Newman ripped at his belt now with both hands, but in reaching for the clasp he forgot about the pistol in his right hand and jammed his finger, still on the trigger. The gun fired directly into the floorboards and the bullet lodged in the armored frame. Lincoln screamed and began to cry, frozen like a small child. The guards swung their guns back to the humvee and threatened to fire but Stirrups leapt in front of them and again screamed in Arabic. Miraculously the guards seemed to relent and Stirrups began to prance around in front of them. The guards laughed and slowly lowered their weapons. The platoon watched in complete and utter bafflement as Stirrups sashayed from one guard to the other and finally stopped, spun, and flopped his wrist at all three guards. They howled with laughter and parted, returning to their posts as Stirrups shuffled back to the humvee smiling to himself.

"What the hell happened in here?" he said as he shut the door behind him.

"The better question is, what the hell happened out there, soldier?" said Newman.

"I don't know, I just started speaking and the words came out… Arabic."

"Exactly!" said Deadweight. "That gas unlocked everything!"

"Hocus-pocus!" screamed Newman. "Stryker here is obviously a bi-lingual."

"A bi-what?" said Stirrups.

"You heard me! And did you have to tell them we were gay? I've got a reputation, you know!"

"In Syria?" said Richards.

"I'm an American general, wise-ass, and that still means something."

"I didn't tell them we were gay," said Stirrups. "I told them we were French."

Newman relented. Embarrassing, but not fatal, he thought. "I suppose that's acceptable," he said. "Though 'French military' is a bit of an oxymoron."

"Oh, don't worry. I didn't claim to be military. I told them we were a French acting troupe. They think we're gypsies."

Newman groaned. The gate arm rose slowly and Richards kept his eyes low as he drove through the checkpoint. The guards waved and laughed as the humvee passed, and Deadweight turned to see them prancing and sashaying around each other as the gate arm slowly lowered between them.

*

Richards brought the humvee to a stop and killed the lights. In front of them sat the rolling sand dunes of the eastern Syrian desert. "Alright, boys," said Newman. "According to mission plan, this is our contact point. Private Richards, contact to occur at zero-five-hundred."

"Roger that," said Richards.

"Time?"

"Zero-four-five-five, General Ginger."

"Contact name?"

"Iad Bin Sussani."

"Lord, that is a mouthful." Newman stepped out of the car and Richards followed. The men shuffled out of the rear seats and spread wide, staying behind to form a perimeter. Newman and Richards approached the foot of the dunes and waited.

"What's the go-word?" asked Newman.

Richards flipped through the brief. "You've got to be kidding me," he said to himself.

"What's the go-word, private?"

"Aubergine."

"What?"

"Aubergine," he repeated, with a distinct edge in his voice.

"What the hell is Aubergine?"

"It's a shade of purple, General," said Richards. "Like plum, but gayer."

"Christ almighty," muttered Newman, before quickly signing the holy trinity and apologizing silently to whoever or whatever was watching from above. It was zero-five-hundred now, and Newman called to the dunes.

"Aubergine. Aubergine."

Newman felt a strange tingle in his belly, as if the mere utterance of the word released some wicked elixir within. His chest tightened and his hand moved to his gun. He was split in two now- he watched himself from a few feet away as he pulled the pistol from his hip. Newman had had this experience before, in The Shit, when it was time to kill. The act of extinguishing another life was so final, so brutal and base that his mind began detaching itself from the mechanical actions of his body, attempting to separate the man from the act in an effort to protect his humanity, and his sanity.

"Aubergine!" called Richards.

Newman watched himself cock the gun, bringing a bullet into the chamber. He wanted to stop himself but something told him to let go, to simply watch, that whatever was happening was right.

"Iad, if you're out there…" Richards's voice trailed off, he could feel Newman staring at him. "Newman?" he said.

Newman watched himself point the gun directly at Richards.

"General, don't do this," said Richards.

Newman watched himself pull the trigger twice. Richards felt the bullets fly past his head and heard two thuds only a few meters behind him. He whipped around to see two men wrapped in black, prone and still clutching machetes.

Newman was suddenly reunited with himself and he quickly lowered the gun. The tingle was gone and he felt weak and nauseous. Someone screamed at him. He looked up and recognized Stirrups, and then Two Strikes, as they wrestled the gun from him. He could see Deadweight and Two Strikes and Lincoln grab Richards. Everyone was angry. There were two dead bodies wrapped in black. Soon he could hear their voices again.

"Have you lost your mind, old man?"

"A couple more steps and Richards would have been…"

"There is no way Ginger could have seen…"

"How did he…"

The men were gathered around Richards and the dead bodies now. Newman was confused. He knew something had happened, but it wasn't his fault, it wasn't General Newman Ginger who had done the thing they were all so mad about. He knew, because he had watched the other guy pull the trigger. He had watched the other General Newman Ginger do it, but the men would never understand.

"Did you see these men?" asked Two Strikes.

"I don't know," he answered truthfully.

"You did," said Richards. "You saw them."

"No," said Newman. "I just sensed them."

"Aubergine!" called a far away voice.

Richards whipped around and drew his gun. "Identify yourself," he screamed, still shaken.

"Aubergine," called the voice, closer now. The man rode camelback down the dune, leading a herd of camels. Flanked by two young boys, who appeared to be shepherds of a sort, the camels loped toward the platoon with complete indifference. It was a relief to Richards, who had grown weary of things coming at him quickly. From the moment he entered the experiment, one thing after another had flown into or around his face and head and psyche, and he frankly could not wait to hop onto one of these dawdling beasts and meander- just meander- to wherever the hell they were supposed to be going.

Newman was awash with embarrassment over his confusion and nausea, he felt like a senile old man, like someone's grandfather dragged along on the family trip out of obligation. He would need to reassert himself as leader of the platoon all over again, he thought. "You Iad?" he called.

"Aubergine, aubergine, yes, yes," said Iad, now close enough to see. Newman sized him up: Kurdish Arab, around 45 with an easy smile and a scruffy, dirty beard. It wasn't until he was a few short meters away that Newman could see the horrific, protruding scar that ran from Iad's temple to the base of his neck.

"You speak American?" asked Newman.

"Ah, General Ginger, I presume."

"Yes, very good."

"Welcome to Zhakoudahouk," he said. Still camel-back, he towered over Newman. "The village elders have prepared a humble meal to welcome your arrival."

"I'm flattered, wish we had time." Newman was tired of arching his neck in order to chat with this camel herder. He felt his old General's swagger rush back. "Boys!" he called. "Mount up!"

Over the next forty minutes, soldier after soldier attempted to mount the ill-proportioned camels. Deadweight carefully laid across its back, between the humps, and fell head first into the sand when the camel stood. Lincoln attempted to sit but fell forward as the camel rose. He wrapped his arms tightly around its long neck, choking and infuriating the beast. The men tried their damnedest not to giggle, but laughter broke out when one of the camels mewled loudly his disapproval of Two Strikes, who sat awkwardly behind the humps, leaning forward and hugging the animal's rib cage.

When he was finally saddled, Newman dug his heels into the camel's ribs and thrust his hips forward, which he was certain was the universal command to move forward quickly. "Hi-ya!" he called. The camel reluctantly strode forward, weighted step after weighted step. Newman, at wit's end, looked to Iad.

"Allah, el Allah," whispered Iad, and rubbed his feet gently against the beast's belly. Without a moment's hesitation, his camel marched away. Newman watched it pass then, furious, dug his heels in even deeper.

"Hi-ya! Hi-ya!" he called.

Newman's camel plodded up the dune and the men followed on their beasts. They whispered to one another about the lope and gait of these exotic, towering creatures.

Stirrups remained behind. He had one of the camel boys hold his mount nearby as he pulled a book of matches from his pack, struck one, and used it to light the entire booklet before tossing it into the open window of the humvee. The flames spread through the interior before devouring the pink coating. He felt the flickering flames and heard the metal twist and squeal as he climbed the dune, but he never looked back.

Chapter 13

Newman ordered one of the camel boys to bring him to the front of the pack, so that he could ride next to Iad. With only a few mumbled words, this waif of a boy prodded the camel into second gear. Newman wasn't certain, but he could have sworn he detected a hint of derision in the young boy's smile. He made a note to censure the boy should the platoon spend any meaningful time in the village.

"Iad," he said. "Iad!"

"Yes, General?"

"How much did central command tell you about this platoon?" he asked. Before he could gauge Iad's response his camel dropped back into first gear and he was quickly ten feet behind Iad. "Dam you, mule!" He dug his heels in again, but the boy placed his hand on the general's foot to stop him. The child then placed his hands on the forward side of the camel's ribcage, mumbled a few hushed words, and in seconds Newman was next to Iad again.

"General," said Iad, "I am but a poor Kurd. I do not wish to know about your platoon, only to help you reach my village, where you may rest and plan the remainder of your mission."

"Does this abomination move any faster?" asked Newman, as he began to fall behind again.

"You westerners take transportation for granted, with your personal cars and paved roads," he said. He rubbed his foot against the camel's ribcage and within a few strides he was slowed, and next to Newman. "These are Allah's chariots, General, a divine blessing. You would be wise to learn…"

"Listen, Iad, there's something funny about these boys," he began.

"I would prefer not to know," interrupted Iad.

"I got a band of brothers that would just as soon be a band of sisters…"

Iad tensed and his camel let out an annoyed grunt. "General, in my country, the offense you suggest is punishable by death," Iad spoke quickly, in clipped tones. "If my villagers kill you, I do not get paid. The CIA has very strict rules about this." Iad rubbed his foot against the camel and pulled ahead.

Newman sunk into his camel and quickly fell behind Iad. The boy kept him in front of the train carrying the platoon, out of respect for his rank. At least someone respected his rank, he thought. Perhaps he would not censure the boy after all. He took in the enormous winter moon, low over the dunes and distant mountains. He had drowned his ability to be moved by natural beauty long ago, washed it out with whiskey, trained himself to immediately find the counterpoint to even the most visceral joys. The moon silhouetting the mountains was gorgeous, he knew that to be true, but to admit it or to verbalize it would chip away at his absolutist illusion that everything in this world was ultimately shit. Instead, at the first internal spark of fascination and wonderment at the natural beauty of this alien terrain, he desperately scrambled through his memory and accumulated knowledge looking for any fragment of evidence that could be used against his natural awe. He came to the poverty and the danger of it all, and the threat of the mission, the unknown nature of the landscape and the people. In short, he came to the fear, and was quickly dispossessed of any bright side. This time, however, the act of seeking the fear seemed strangely superficial. Perhaps it was the stress, or the headaches that had grown progressively worse since the testing, or perhaps it was the lack of booze- that fog that rolled in nightly to cloud the day and obscure all thoughts of tomorrow- its absence had cleared the way for some heightened awareness of his own processes, he thought. Who knows. Whatever the reason, he was now inside his own head, a spectator as much as a participant, and he didn't like it. He felt, for the first time, a tinge of shame at his own desperation to sully something so beautiful as the crystalline night sky against these ancient mountains. These mountains, that moon, those stars. They were survivors, he thought. He and his boys would come and go, the villagers, the wars, the races and the animals would ebb and flow and eventually turn to dust while this mountain and this moon and these stars watched from their perches, surviving. Perhaps they were the warriors, he thought. Or perhaps they were God. Perhaps they looked down and scoffed at us childish, base animals warring for scraps of land and food like the cosmic ants we are. What wisdom they must have then, having seen so much already. What would they tell us, he thought? Probably nothing. Why bother? They would turn to one another and say, simply, "Here they go again." He smiled at the thought of a shrugging, yawning mountain rolling its eyes to the moon and the stars as the humans below unleashed nuclear bombs and vile diseases and thrashed and raped and pillaged across the earth. He sided with the mountain.

This was new for him, this thought that perhaps it was all a little silly. He was a career general, a history buff, a student of war. Was he betraying his life's work by being so… what? Open, maybe? Was it anathema for a man of his pedigree to be open to the possibility that they all had it wrong, every one of them, every general, every commander, every president and prime minister and king and queen throughout the ages? Was he a traitor to his life's work, to his government, to his military for considering the idea that the silent mountain, the distant moon and the infinite stars were the deities, to be ignored at the world's peril?

His mind was spent. The rhythmic lope of the camel was pounding sleep into his head and shoulders, and he allowed himself to doze off with the promise of returning to this at some later time, with a glass of whiskey and closed shades.

*

Automatic gunfire slammed into the night sky above Newman's head and he nearly leapt from the camel. He twisted and turned to find his boys, he thought he would have to track the edges of the visible world to see them scrambling from the ambush but they loped along behind him still. They wore expressions of various levels of concern, but to Newman's surprise no one was running for cover or drawing a weapon. He breathed deeply and looked forward again, just as another round of automatic gunfire clapped into the sky. Dozens of Kurds waited a few hundred meters ahead, guns raised into the air. Even the women and children appeared to be armed and firing into the sky. It was either an ambush or the world's most terrifying welcome ceremony.

Ahead, Iad dismounted as the Kurdish men greeted him. They fired into the air again and Newman wondered where the hundreds of rounds came from, and just as importantly, where they would land in a few moments. These Kurds seemed to punctuate a sentence by popping off a few rounds, he thought. Every five god damn seconds they would throw their guns into the air and squeeze off enough rounds to tear through the entire platoon and their camels to boot. The women and children appeared to follow suit for no apparent reason other than to feel busy, he thought, and if this is how they celebrated, how the hell did they argue?

Iad gestured toward Newman and the platoon as the camel boys led them down the small slope leading into the village. The men abruptly turned and vanished into the darkened alleys, and the women and children followed. Iad turned to Newman and smiled that apologetic shrug of a smile one uses in such circumstances. Before Newman could ask about the sentiments of the villagers Iad was whisking the men down from their camels and barking orders at the camel boys. Newman was groggy and fell in line as he and the platoon were shown through the alleys and open dirt and stone patches that comprised the village, which was little more than a pastiche of huts and bombed out, one-story buildings the size of small apartments. He was too exhausted to take his rightful place at the front of the line, but rationalized it was so dark and so late the men would hardly notice.

The men laid their packs down inside the stone square and looked around. The air was thin. Iad explained this would be their base camp from which to launch the rescue mission and Newman thanked him and showed him out, with plans to meet at zero-six-hundred for a full debriefing on the terrain and the extraordinarily limited resources available to them.

Newman estimated it was three in the morning before the villagers had all retired for the evening, because that's when the intermittent gunfire seemed to stop for good. He was pleased to think about silence for the next three or four hours. But a funny thing happened when he tried to close his eyes: he saw General Fuller staring back at him. Fuller's mouth twisted into his infamously bastardized smile and Newman heard himself begging the general for something. He was pleading, yelling. He needed more time, he heard himself say. He watched a silhouette of himself kneel in front of the son of a bitch. Fuller's eyes darkened but the crook in the lips remained, and all he said was, "good luck, old man."

Newman wasn't sure where he was going, but he knew it would give him more time. His head pounded. The blood vessels constricted through his temples and every heartbeat echoed in his ears. He stumbled through the village toward the only escape he could think of- he had seen the camel boys tie the beasts to a few posts near an opening in the maze of huts and stone. He could barely form a complete thought and he had to shuffle through fragments to make sense of each step forward. He kept hearing the refrain, "more time" and each time he felt a surge forward, a burst of adrenaline toward those hideous, complacent things, the camels. He heard a mewling, crowing whine and when he opened his eyes he was bouncing along a trail in the valley of two massive dunes. The world spun and he cursed himself for being drunk again. He remembered just before his eyes closed again that he had not had a sip in days and days. He scolded himself in a dream for being so short with his wife that morning and awoke to see the black sky turning grey-blue and the camel trotting dangerously fast. He needed more time, more time before the sun rose and revealed him to this new world, he thought, they would string him alive, they would draw and quarter him. He closed his eyes and felt himself come undone, he was out of time, he knew.

Chapter 14

Richards snatched the bowl of hummus from Cruz and hurled it at the wall. The small wooden bowl shattered into a dozen pieces and sent dip everywhere. "Was it that bad?" said Cruz.

"What?" barked Richards. "Oh, the hummus? The hummus was fine, Cruz, thank you." Richards was steamed over Newman's disappearance. It was high noon, and he had been missing since at least daybreak, when Richards first awoke and noticed the platoon numbered only six. The men unanimously believed he went AWOL, but Richards held fast to the argument that he must be out scouting, gathering intelligence, doing some good old-fashioned reconnaissance. Stirrups found it laughable that the bumbling, stumbling old man would be crawling through the hills spying on anyone or anything, except maybe a few desert shrubs. The old fart disappeared in the middle of the night, stole a camel and took off into the desert, plain and simple, argued Stirrups. Newman was nuts, and good riddance. Day had broken and they were losing time, he argued, but Richards just stared out that hole in the stone wall, convinced the old bastard was coming back for his men.

"Maybe that's my new power," said Cruz. "Maybe I make good dips."

"It'll be bigger than that," said Richards. "Trust me."

"Trust you?" said Stirrups. "You haven't done a god damn thing since Ginger went AWOL. Why should we trust you?"

"He's coming back! A General does not abandon his troops. Especially not a General who's been hit by that gas."

"But he wasn't hit," said Lincoln. "The canister broke his nose, and…"

"My ass," barked Stryker.

"We were all hit, Lincoln," said Richards. "Every one of us. And we're all on our way to something great, even Newman Ginger."

"How come you got such a hard on for him, anyways," said Two Strikes between pushups across the room.

"Because that's all I got, okay? I was just a soldier before, and maybe now I'm gonna be a great soldier. And a great soldier is loyal, even in the face of all this doubt."

"You're second in command," said Stirrups. "You take over. You're here now. We'll follow you."

"If it's real, if we were all hit," said Lincoln, "how come it hasn't happened to me?"

"It is happening," said Richards, "just at a different pace for everyone. I've wanted to be a real soldier my entire life. But I was too slow, too soft, too stupid. Ever since we got hit with that gas, we've been bigger, stronger, faster, smarter. But if it's possible, even for a second, that one of us didn't get gay from that gas, then it's possible none of us did. And I, for one, am not willing to believe that this is all some big lie." Brooklyn knelt down to take a break from his pushups. He could sense the longing in Richard's voice. Deadweight sat up in bed, troubled by the thought that this could all be a passing moment, or a vanishing gift to be grown out of. Richards continued, "I trust my body, and every inch of it tells me that I have some new power, that you have some new power, and that yes, even General Newman Ginger has some new power, some new gift. It may take months or even years, but when he's ready…" His voice trailed off, as if it was a stretch of logic to believe that Newman Ginger would display some clear positive change from that gas, and his newfound sexuality. In truth, Richards doubted only himself. This was a symptom of his long-held belief that he was ever so slightly less than. Perhaps it was a result of being the youngest, the runt of the litter, or perhaps it was a byproduct of hearing the magnificent war stories of his father and uncles and grandfather as a child, and thinking the world had enough heroes, and there must be some magical alchemy in those men that made them heroes. He never allowed for the possibility that adults self-aggrandized, lied, touted or bragged. He never asked for the details, the little shades of truth that turn gods into mortals and heroism into duty. He failed to see that the true gift of the men around him was not battlefield prowess, which was shared with thousands of other brave warriors in every instance, but the ability to carve away at the slow, trudging fat of life and present an audience with only the leanest, most delectable bits of the recounted moment. In short, they could tell one hell of a story. But Richards was a gifted listener, a wide-eyed doe, the perfect audience for blowhards and sages alike, and instead of developing a voice he developed only a sympathetic ear and marginal self-esteem. This moment, in front of his downtrodden men, was the closest he had ever come to leading and certainly the first speech he had ever delivered. He took the deadened eyes and shifting bottoms to mean failure, and he wasn't far off. He had set the men on a course of thought focused primarily upon all the reasons they must be deluded to believe they were metamorphosing into something profound thanks to some silly purple gas. Physical evidence aside, each man still floated somewhere between wary acceptance, baffled experimentation, and flustered denial in Newman's case. With such a terrifying mission ahead, the last thing any of them needed was more reason to doubt their new, suspect ability to run, jump, shoot and win.

Automatic gunfire spat in the distance. Richards peered through the hole in the hut and saw movement in the distance.

"What's going on?" asked Lincoln.

"Maybe it's someone's birthday," said Stirrups, sarcastically.

"Or a wedding," cracked Deadweight.

"Or a funeral," said Cruz, warily. But the sounds of celebration filtered through the maze of huts and stone, coupled with more gunfire.

"Or Newman," said Richards.

*

The men sprinted toward the commotion in various states of undress. Richards flicked off the safety on his gun. As he turned the corner his stomach fell. Draped across the humps of a large, mewling camel was Newman, passed out or dead, he couldn't be sure. Villagers pulled him from the beast and he fell to the ground headfirst. They tugged at his arms and legs and fired their guns into the air. Iad watched from a safe distance and Richards ran to him.

"What the hell is happening?"

"We have caught a thief."

"Let go of him!" yelled Richards. "Tell them to let go of him!"

"It is in Allah's hands now," said Iad, with a callous shrug.

Richards shoved through the clamoring Kurds. "Let go of him!"

The platoon pulled anyone they could grab from the crazed mob and worked their way toward Newman. The Kurds were like a starved pack of wolves picking at a felled deer. Richards reached the camel and wedged himself between two young men who gave way without much resistance, as if they weren't particularly hungry for this. Richards was shocked at how easily they quit and shuffled off, as if they would follow whoever yelled the loudest at any given moment. He quickly decided to pursue this tact and screamed. "Stop! Stop now!" he shouted. He fired his pistol into the air but the Kurds took this as a rallying cry and fired their guns into the air again, and bellowing a strange, guttural howl. Richards wrestled one of Newman's ankles from a clawing Kurdish woman and looked for his platoon mates. They were busy pushing through, throwing men out of the throng and shoving women and children aside. Suddenly Iad was upon him, screaming in a mix of Arabic and English about stealing camels and Allah and justice. "Tell them to let him go" Richards screamed back. "Tell them now!" Stirrups was next through the mob, and he immediately yelled at Iad, in what seemed to be Arabic as he wrested Newman's arm from a small, fat Kurdish woman in full veil. What had been Newman's black and blue nose and eyes were now a sallow, sunken yellow. Iad took turns screaming at Richards and Stirrups. A small Kurd appeared next to Iad, an old man, and began growling at both Iad and Stirrups. "What the hell is he saying?" yelled Richards.

"He says the camel is sacred," screamed Iad. "Mohammed rode the camel from Medina to Mecca. You steal a camel, you offend both man and Allah." The old man raised a bony finger and made some garbled pronouncement and suddenly the mob went wild, and pressed forward, reaching over each other to brush and pat the elder. Those closest to Newman began to pull at his shirt buttons and belt.

"What did he say?" yelled Richards. Before Iad could answer the elder reached into his baggy sleeve and pulled out a small pistol and pointed it at Newman, still stretched between the two soldiers and the Kurds.

"The punishment for offending Allah is death!" called Iad. Stirrups screamed at him in clicks and consonants as the elder intoned a prayer and cocked the hammer. The mob pressed forward again, thirsty for spilled blood.

Without a thought, Richards dropped Newman, pulled his pistol from his waistband and leveled the gun to the camel's head. "Any of you fucking move, and I will spread this thing's brains all over the fucking place," he screamed.

The mob fell silent and the elder lowered his gun slowly. Two Strikes shouldered his way through the mob and grabbed the general from the Kurds, and threw the limp body over his shoulder. He turned and bowled through the crowd, escorted by Lincoln and Cruz, and they disappeared into the twists and turns of the village.

The camel, clueless that he stood teetering on the precipice of death, sniffed the gun and grunted, as if dismissing rotten fruit at the market. The noise jarred Richards, who had all but forgotten he was currently holding a gun directly to the head of an innocent camel. He took a quick inventory of the situation, as if he had just arrived, and realized that at some point, he may have to shoot this thing. He looked for Iad, but caught only a sliver of the mercenary as he disappeared into the alleys of the village.

"Stirrups, get them out of here," he called, and gestured toward the mob. But Stirrups had little to do. It seemed many of the Kurds had no real conviction about the camel thievery, or perhaps no knowledge of it, as the edges of the mob frayed and disappeared into the huts and stone. They were simply here for the show, Richards realized. But that left the matter of the camel-hostage, and its owners, to whom Richards apologized profusely through Stirrups' inexplicable

Arabic, with his gun safely lodged in his belt and away from the oblivious beast. On the jog back to their hut, Richards was troubled by his apparent willingness to murder the clunky, disinterested animal, but his horror was tempered by the knowledge that he had had the best intentions in doing so.

Chapter 15

Iad could barely hide his agitation. He had spent hours on camelback to get to Kuwait and now he was forced to sit and wait outside General Sydney 'Bird Dog' Fuller's office for equally as long. He barely knew this man, Bird Dog, but he resented having to deal with someone of such low status in the American system. Some random minion from deep within the defense department? After all he had done for the U.S., not only on his current mission, but on dozens of missions past… It was Iad who had first introduced the tall, gaunt defense official to Hussein's inner circle when the defense official wanted to arm the dictator with heavy weapons, planes and munitions back in '83. It was Iad who later provided safe-houses for U.S. Special Forces in the lead up to Desert Storm, in such hostile territories as Basra and Bussayyah, a turn that led to his eventual exile by Hussein, come to think of it, which sent him back home to the Kurdish north, to live three huts down from his mother and father, and grandmother,

Allah bless her soul. And more recently, it was Iad who tipped off his U.S. contacts to Saddam Hussein's tiny nuclear arms cache, though he could never pinpoint exactly where the three catastrophic missiles were safe-guarded. He couldn't prove their existence either, which had cost him some standing in the U.S. intelligence community, another slap in the face for loyal friend Iad, he thought. And after all this, he was still made to sit and wait, like some servant or woman. Yes, this entire ordeal had become quite a nuisance. He should have known better. When dealing with the U.S. military nowadays there were always so many hoops to jump through when you wanted to kill someone. The paperwork alone disincentivized a man from pursuing what used to be a simple matter of assembling a mob and pointing. In the old days, he thought. In the old days, before cable television and the new thing, the Internet, a man could smite his enemies, or stone a rival at will. And honor killings! Whatever happened to honor killings of besmirched wives and daughters, he wondered wistfully to himself. "The general will see you now," said the secretary. Iad snuck a quick peek at her exposed ankles and immediately felt guilty. He muttered "Allah, forgive me," to himself, stood, took a deep breath and marched into the general's office.

"I demand justice," he said.

"Sit down," Fuller commanded, nonplussed. Iad sat.

"One of your men, the leader, he stole a camel and rode off into the night!"

"Go on."

"He would have gotten away with it, but he was unprepared for the desert heat, and passed out soon after sunrise.

"Dead?" asked Fuller, with just a hint of hope in his voice.

"No! The camel, unaccustomed to this rider, this thief, turned around and trotted home."

"Interesting. Say, how fast is a camel?"

"It tops out around 25 kilometers per hour."

Fuller raised an eyebrow ever so slightly. That was a good ten kilometers per hour faster than he had anticipated.

"Sir," continued Iad, "When the man was moments from justice, a soldier in his unit…" Iad's voice trailed off. The memory was almost too painful to recount. "A soldier in his unit placed a gun to the camel's head, and ordered the release of his leader. Stealing a camel is a sin against man and God! Placing a gun to its head, killing it would be..."

Fuller swung his chair the final few inches to face Iad squarely. He could give a shit about the camel, he thought, or whatever else this sweaty, dirt-encrusted towel-head was blabbing about, but there were trouble signs in that tale. The leader, probably General Ginger, looked to escape: he didn't buy into the suicide mission. Further, one of his underlings took dramatic steps to (successfully) keep the platoon together: he was bonding to the unit, and keeping the men alive. Too many variables, he thought. Even the best laid plans. He would have to accelerate to the end game, total annihilation. He realized Iad was saying something, still speaking.

"And for that reason, I would like your permission to assassinate..."

"Fine."

"Fine?"

"Yes, yes. In fact," said Fuller, as he leaned forward, "I have a little secret for you. Iad, how do your people feel about homosexuality?"

Iad stiffened. He had been approached by American military personnel before, even succumbed on a couple lonely nights in the cold, vast desert, but he found this approach to be rather forward. "It is a sin against man and God," he barked reflexively.

"Good, good. You know, Iad, we're not so different, you and I. Now, what if I was to tell you that entire platoon was merely a gaggle of homosexuals, parading around as United States military men? What then?"

Iad remembered the general's pleading on that first night, something about a band of sisters. He had refused to hear it then, and he refused to hear it now. Fuller was perplexed.

"What's the problem?"

"Sir, if my people discover they are housing and feeding homosexuals, in their very own village, they will form a mob, hunt the men down, and stone them to death."

"And?"

"I don't want that on my conscience," said Iad. He feigned a sincere, concerned looked as best he could, but something in his voice registered with Fuller. Perhaps it was that word, conscience. Iad's voice had flown up a full octave on that word, as if his subconscious and his throat had conspired to restrict its passage, knowing it was horseshit. Yes, thought Fuller, according to his dossier this Iad character was a career mercenary, a local fixer for hire. If he knew the word "conscience" he knew it solely as a tool, like a gun or cash, to be kept in his back pocket until a the moment dictated its usage.

"Would your *conscience* be eased at all if you were paid upfront for this mission?"

"Considerably."

"Fine. Those men are fags, queer as a cantaloupe. Do what you will with that information. There will be a small briefcase with twenty five thousand dollars at the front desk for you. Good day." Fuller stood and extended his hand.

"Make it Euros," said Iad. "The dollar is worth shit over here."

Chapter 16

Stirrups lifted the small boulder like it was a throw pillow, set it on his shoulder and walked carefully toward the hut at the edge of the village. Cruz followed, with a massive slab pulled from the rubble of one of the many bombed out huts. In the distance, Lincoln and Two Strikes dug through collapsed walls for usable barriers as Deadweight leapt from roof to roof, or whatever remained of them and scanned the rubble from above.

"Let's go, boys," called Richards. "Thirty minutes to sundown!" He studied a topographical map of the region and was chagrined to learn there wasn't a flat surface within 500 miles. No safe approach, no safe escape, all peaks and valleys and terrain. He allowed the men to distract him for a moment. Each carried hundreds of pounds of stone like it was a prop made of foam. They tugged and lifted and carried clumps of rock with inhuman ease, and laughed along the way, cracking jokes, sharing stories. They were growing stronger, smoother.

Each slab was deposited at points around the hut, to fortify what would become base camp for the rescue mission. Richards made the decision to entrench the hut following the morning's nightmarish encounter with local justice. Once you put a gun to a man's camel, your peaceful stay in his village is limited, he thought.

Richards tensed as Newman scuttled across the courtyard toward him. He had been remanded to bed and given an IV drip by Lincoln, the platoons de facto medic, and Richards hoped the men could finish securing the hut before he had to deal with the old man again. But here he came, his hair wild and greasy, caked with sweat and sand, and his uniform in tatters, buttons undone, boots untied. His eyes were bloodshot, as if coming off a crying jag.

"I've done it, Richards," he cooed.

"What have you done, general?" Richards studied the old man's eyes as they darted back and forth. This skittish, wounded General Ginger was a stranger to him.

"That gas," he said. "I know what it did to you. Do you know what it did to me?" He had a glint in his eyes, a flash of excitement like lightning.

"What did it do to you, general?"

"It released me, Richards. While you boys slowly turn into the men you were destined to be, so, too, do I."

"You're turning gay?" Richards' voice cracked as the words crawled out.

"I am turning into General George S. Patton," he growled. He frantically scanned Richard's eyes for a response, but the young man did not speak. "Well?" he demanded.

Richards glanced around to make sure the men did not hear their general's psychotic ramblings. Though they carried slabs the size of boulders and leapt from building to building they were his reality, they were his anchor to sanity and he needed them focused and comfortable. Their boat had been rocked enough to last them a lifetime, he didn't need Newman's demise to capsize it completely before the mission had even begun. "What?" was all he could muster.

"Maybe you boys were destined to become great queens, but I was destined to become a great general. I feel him inside me, Richards. Did you know I was born on the day he died? December twenty-first, 1945. I never told anyone this before, because-" He peered over his shoulder to make sure they were alone, then leaned into Richards. "Frankly, I was worried it might make me sound crazy." He flashed a quick, conspiratorial smile. "But I have always suspected a little piece of that man's soul left his body that day and wound up in mine."

Richards felt himself breathe for the first time in minutes. His heart pounded. This wasn't so bad, he thought. Ginger had lost it, but men become shell-shocked in battle. He had been prosthelytized to before, in the shit of training once. Overcome by heat and the vicious mock-shelling they were undergoing, one man attempted to convert him as they lay in a foxhole, another blathered on about seeing the Archangel Michael in the barracks the night before. Harmless rants, the windy disposal of pent up tension. At least he didn't do anything stupid, thought Richards, like steal another camel. He tried to suppress a smile.

Newman sensed the kid pull away. He knew this moment well. He saw the interest- the fear, really- slip from Richards' eyes and suddenly Newman was the soaking wet drunk regaling the young men at the bar with war stories and conquests, a wobbly, shameful old sot who had been humored long enough. Not today, he thought.

"You don't believe me," said Newman. His face tightened. "Come see for yourself."

A chill ran down Richards' spine. That word, "see." Come "see" for yourself. Nothing good could come of this, he knew, and he steeled himself for a very long afternoon.

Newman led Richards into the barracks hut and flung open the makeshift curtain that separated the hut from the latrine. There, standing atop a cinderblock, stark naked and blindfolded was the village elder. A few feet away a car battery sat on the stone floor with small red, white and blue wires connecting it to the old man's scrotum. As the elder shivered, Richards could see the wires were attached to the wrinkled, sagging skin with small metallic clamps that reflected slivers of light from the single overhead bulb.

"He's about to break," said Newman. "I can feel it."

Richards gripped the wall for support. Things happened very quickly now. More men entered. Richards could tell they were platoon members, so they were safe for now. There was shouting. Newman fiddled with the car battery until someone punched him in the nose again. Richards kneeled down at some point, for a few moments, to steady himself. When he stood the village elder was gone, carried to the hillside behind the village and left hooded but unchained by Lincoln and Cruz, who decided in a moment of panic masquerading as inspiration that it would be best to confuse the elder further. They agreed the less sense his story made, the greater chance it would be dismissed as the insane, paranoid doddering of an old man.

The world began to slow down. Richards could make out individual faces and voices. There was an air of hysteria inside the hut as these large, carved bodies slammed into one another, tearing off their thobes and throwing supplies into their packs. Everyone moved too quickly, arguing over what to do with the general, what to do about the elder, what to do, what to do...

"Attention!" screamed Richards. "Attention!"

The men froze. The word came out closer to someone calling for help than leading an elite fighting unit. Richards had never screamed at anyone before, had never bossed anyone about, or commanded anything of anyone and he was genuinely shocked to see the platoon members halt. Who would listen to him, he thought? What the hell did he know?

Richards surveyed the doe-eyed group while they stared back and awaited the very next thought to spill out of his mouth. They resembled children as much as soldiers, he thought, the way they sincerely and intensely awaited instruction. They were, after all, young men, as was he. The only man over 30 in the group was lying prone on the floor bleeding from a thrice-broken nose after losing his mind and stealing camels and old men. Their de facto leader had turned into a nut case, Richards realized and now it was youth leading youth, or, more accurately, the blind leading the blind. It was a disheartening thought, but it was the truth, he knew. If they were children he would have to be their father, if they were soldiers he would have to be their commanding officer. As his boys stared back at him, Richards decided he must have a next thought. You commanded their attention for a reason, he told himself, don't keep them waiting.

"Okay," he began. "Here's what we're going to do," he continued, without any notion of what they were going to do.

At that exact moment, Lincoln burst in through the front door of the hut. All heads turned to face him, grateful for the break in the lengthy awkward silences that defined Richards' rein so far.

"What's the matter?" asked Richards.

"I think you should look outside," panted Lincoln.

The men darted to the small square holes that passed for windows. In the distance, at the end of the long corridor of devastated stone and thatch huts a small, dancing fire crept toward them. The men studied the blaze. Curiously, the fire did not grow as it overtook hut after hut. The dragon had no tail.

As it turned the corner, only 200 meters away, the men could see quite plainly the reason for this: the fire was actually the top half of a mob of torch-wielding Kurds, marching toward the barracks, led by one Iad bin-al Sussani.

Chapter 17

The armored envoy rolled past the sign reading, "United States Central Command, Kuwait," which sat atop the sign reading, "Visitors Will Be Shot." Deichmann was certain he was the only person in this group who noticed the mistake, but now, he reasoned, was not the time to bring up the semantic difference between "visitors" and "trespassers." How this had slipped through the Signage Tracking Division was beyond him, he thought, before recalling that the Signage Tracking Division had been dissolved and all sign-making and sign-correcting duties were now subcontracted out to a subsidiary of America's largest defense contractor, Signage Tracking Delivery, at quadruple the cost and one-tenth the competency.

Deichmann bristled at the notion that some private company was brought in to flub up the perfectly decent job our men and women were doing, but, he thought, the Pentagon must have its reasons. What he couldn't know was the Pentagon's only reason for contracting Signage Tracking Delivery was that a top Pentagon official had retired, joined the board of Signage Tracking Delivery, and then proposed to his old colleagues in the Pentagon that they contract the Signage Tracking Delivery company to do the tedious work of sign-making and sign-correcting themselves, thereby alleviating the military's obvious signage burden. It would, of course, cost a little more than keeping signage in-house, but it would increase efficiency and focus, and could the Pentagon really put a price on increased efficiency and focus? The Pentagon decided that the price of increased efficiency and focus was in the neighborhood of 1.2 billion dollars each year, exactly four times the sign-making and sign-correcting costs incurred by the military's own signage division, and Signage Tracking Delivery was officially and irrevocably contracted by the United States Armed Forces. The former Pentagon official was suddenly rich beyond his wildest dreams and the signs that adorned every tent, structure and corner of army bases around the world were suddenly rife with errors, incongruities, misspellings and poor grammar, for one of the hallmarks of Signage Tracking Delivery- and their parent company- were the zero-liability clauses built into their devilishly rich contracts. They reasoned, quite successfully, that if they were going to do the military the thankless favor of taking over its most boring and drab jobs, they should be compensated for the drabness. Further, they argued, they often had to do these jobs in some nasty countries, after all. It's not like the military only needed signs in Honolulu, or Charleston. Signage Tracking Delivery would have to send men and women everywhere the military sent men and women, and that costs serious money, and civilians don't always like living in Berlin, or Kuwait, and they would need to be compensated for the inconvenience, on top of the boredom of the job itself. And finally, they argued, how could such inconvenienced and bored civilians be expected to get every sign right all the time? It's not like they had undergone rigorous military training, and were accustomed to the selfless accountability of military service. To subject them to the same standard of performance that a United States soldier was subjected to, for instance, would be absurd and probably bad for morale. Instead, this former top Pentagon official argued, the zero-liability clause would keep spirits high and signs on-time, and the slightly-younger current top Pentagon officials seemed to agree with the slightly-older former top Pentagon official, and Signage Tracking Delivery was granted the same zero-liability clause as their parent company usually was, and many handshakes and slaps on the back were shared by all as the first annual 1.2 billion dollar invoice was passed from former to current top Pentagon officials. The former top Pentagon official was so delighted he even offered a select handful of the current top Pentagon officials who had facilitated the contracting of Signage Tracking Delivery senior management positions at Signage Tracking Delivery upon their eventual retirement from the public sector.

Deichmann knew none of this, of course, only that he was miserable, sandwiched between Burnam and Fuller in the back of the black sport utility vehicle, dismayed by the poor signage outside the vehicle and the weak air conditioning inside. Conversation had been wanting. Burnam showed up to the hangar raging drunk and proceeded to pass out upon takeoff. He awoke when he pissed himself during a steep drop in altitude, Deichmann noted, first by his waking gasp, and then by the smell of damp piss. He was shocked to see Burnam then pull a flask from his duffel, but grateful that the general would soon be asleep again. The day only tumbled downhill from there, as the cold, rude General Fuller picked them up at the airport. Deichmann got the distinct feeling that Fuller wanted to kill him. He resolved to stay alert, but knew the brute could overtake him at will. Should he encounter Fuller in a dark alley his only hope would be to outsmart or outrun the monster. There were a lot of dark alleys at CentCom Kuwait, Deichmann knew, because these bases were built hastily, with additions being thrown up all the time, like temporary barracks and bunkers and mess halls. Worried that Fuller would pick up on his plotting, Deichmann attempted to behave inconspicuously on the ride from the airport to CentCom Kuwait, so he was left to clutch his bag and glance through the tinted windows of the sport utility vehicle. The passing sand, forever sand, left him little to work with, however and he soon resorted to staring straight ahead through the front of the vehicle. The problem, he soon realized was that Fuller, too, was looking straight ahead, and they both rested in the other's peripheral vision, which would certainly draw Fuller's attention to him, and his to Fuller before long. So Deichmann did the only logical thing, and tilted his head back, and stared directly at the roof for the remainder of the ride.

Fuller swallowed what felt like a bullet of dust-covered mucus. The sand and dry heat was murder on his sinuses. It was adding injury to insult, he thought, sending him to this scorching third-world shitbox to oversee this absurd mission. He had been here three days and already he wanted to strangle everyone and everything he came in contact with. He certainly wanted to strangle this idiot in a lab coat crammed next to him, staring at the roof, muttering to himself. At least he didn't have to deal with the slobbering old fool asleep in the other corner. By the time Burnam dried out it would all be over and he could hop the next plane home, good riddance to these assholes and good riddance to this byzantine sweatbox.

Between the self-pitying and the bloodlust, however, Fuller did have one reasonable thought. What in the hell was the doctor doing here? If the mission is proceeding as planned, and those faggots are on their way out, he thought, what's the point of bringing the egghead and the drunk all the way out here? Something was up, he knew, and as the senior officer on the project, this could mean only one thing: more work. Not good, thought Fuller. Not good.

*

Cadbury marched through Hallway U-7, seven stories under the sand, and seven stories closer to the oil that made this little beach nation with inhospitable shores and unswimmable water such a sought after destination for him and his contemporaries. With each descendant floor he could feel the plodding, churning energy of it. Sinclair's black goo, the Sheiks' and Mullahs' lifeblood and birthright, the engine of the world stirred beneath him. So he walked. He walked the nine stories down the strictly right-angled hallways, chopping their way into the earth, through sand and sand and sand and eventually bedrock. He walked to absorb through osmosis the energy of the earth, that which both caused and fueled brutal, inhumane wars of scale, and wars of the world, that put entire nations, entire civilizations at risk. Even at 60 he wanted to be where the action was. So he walked.

By the time he reached his office on U-9 he was practically reverberating from all the energy he had absorbed on his nine-floor walk. He briefly considered taking the elevator up to 1 and walking down the nine floors again, but his heart could not take it, quite literally: his hypertension left him with great risk of a stroke, or worse, and often these nine-story struts with all the rich oil energy spilling into his system left him completely spent. Why tempt fate, he thought? Besides, he had a feeling this "urgent" meeting with that doctor from the O.C.D. experiment would most certainly increase his blood pressure by double digits, and probably undo everything the walk and the oil osmosis had done… He was furious before he even entered the room. That was another side effect of all the unprocessed petrol seeping into his consciousness, he knew: mood swings. For years he marked these swings, and did his absolute best to contain them and their attendant effects, but that too became exhausting, and eventually he simply had to decide between being reasonable and measured or being himself- himself, alive and spinning with natural oil energy- and for the good of the United States he decided to drop the filter and simply let rip. He had broken more than a few spirits in the intervening years, he knew, but he had also been responsible for launching many wars, covert and broadcast, so you tell me, he thought, you tell me.

"Welcome to Kuwait, gentlemen," he said as he burst into the room. The doctor and the drunk sprang out of their seats and belched out the best salute that could be expected from such clowns. Fuller, noted Cadbury, was perfectly erect, stiff as a board with brilliant phrasing in his short, curt salute.

"Doctor, what is this emergency?" asked Cadbury.

Deichmann shifted in his seat and held reams of paper to his chest. They were not organized in any particular manner, in fact they were not meant to be presented. The critical data he came to share was scattered throughout the clutch, of course, but he knew if he simply handed Cadbury such unfiltered, undigested information it would be treated with the same disregard as the men whose physiology it described in precise account. No, it was not to be handed over, it was to be held onto, held tightly just under his quivering chin, a five-inch thick buffer between him and the brutes, between reason and insanity, humanity and avarice. It was his armor, and more truthfully, it was his security blanket.

"I…" he began. "*We* have a growing concern about confidence levels in the O.C.D. declared results." He looked directly at Cadbury, knowing the wicked general to his left and the soaked general to his right wanted only to get as far away from this sequestered office in this inferno of a nation as possible. Their only growing concern was lunch and the next plane to Germany.

"There is a confidence concern?" said Cadbury.

"Correct, sir."

"What is our current confidence status?"

"Lack thereof, sir."

"Specifically?"

"General Newman Ginger, sir." Deichmann paused. He knew the name carried special significance in this small circle, for the general was the oldest, most experienced of the subjects. Fuller knew him well, though no love appeared to have been lost between the two men. He was simply the expected anomaly, should one appear, and more to the point, he was the closest in age and stature to the three decorated men in the room. They could see themselves in him, if they could see themselves in anybody, Deichmann had calculated, and thus he also stood the best chance of reprieve.

"Denial," said Cadbury.

"So we thought…" began Deichmann.

"The man doth protest too much."

"Perhaps with good reason, sir!"

"Yeah, nobody wants to be gay," offered Fuller.

Deichmann could feel the meeting slipping through his fingers. "Sir, physically and mentally this entire platoon tested in the 112th percentile," he pleaded. "Literally, off the charts."

"Adrenaline does wonders," said Cadbury. "Outliers. Flukes."

"Sir, they display an almost superhuman capability. We don't understand it yet, but something quite magical is happening with these men."

"Fascinating, doctor," said Cadbury. "But ultimately academic. Our hands will be scrubbed of this stain in a matter of days."

"But sir, that brings me to the curious case of General Newman Ginger." He leaned forward to suggest there was something both secretive and urgent about the matter, and he thought he recognized a glimmer of interest flash through Cadbury's eyes. "An utter failure by all accounts, he is by no means as… capable as the rest of the platoon. But if, in fact, General Ginger's nose was broken in the initial test, there is a very real possibility that the olfactory receptor cells were never activated, that his mucosal membrane was, in fact, latent, and never stimulated, and that he is, in fact, therefore, subsequently, still…" he paused and watched as Cadbury's head turned ever so slightly, to square with his own. "…a heterosexual."

For the first time since he entered the room, Cadbury was silent. Deichmann could hear himself pant. His heart raced. He was embroiled in the first fight of his life, and it exhilarated him. He rarely interacted with others, let alone argued with them. He had certainly never spoken back, not to his mother or father, not to any teacher, and of course not to a superior in the United States armed forces. But here he was, he marveled, going a few rounds with the Secretary of Defense himself.

He pulled himself back from the ledge, reminding himself that he signed up for this over two decades ago, for the exacting stringency and structure that now stifled him. He was a simple boy who grew into a simple man, and the will and confidence of others- first at home and then in the service- had always provided a very simple path for him to glide along, and for that he was always grateful. But something about this moment, something about this man's tone was stuck in his ear, bouncing off the walls of his brain, picking up size and momentum. It wasn't the words, he thought, no. He'd heard the words before. He'd heard "no" before, many times over this twenty-year career, and he'd grown grateful for even that, for "no" was a structure unto itself. It meant turn away, turn back, try again, do not proceed. It was a continuance of the structure, albeit in a disheartening direction. But was he disheartened now, he wondered? No. He was… angry.

Anger is such an ugly trait, he knew. Anger makes people ugly because they lose control, they say rude things. They act out. They bring attention to themselves, and their wants. That was the hideousness narcissism of anger, he thought: it propelled people to express themselves, to vocalize out of turn. What would happen to The Structure if everyone spoke out of turn? The thought seized him with panic. A world of angry people speaking out of turn was a world of chaos, of unpredictability. Who knows what the people will want tomorrow, or suddenly, now? Who wants to know? Utter chaos, he knew. Order came from submission of the self, of the wants, of the desires. He was in the military, he was in the Order business.

Yet… the anger only grew. Between Cadbury's breaths he scanned the contents of his soul, searching for the origin of this bitter, seizing anger. It was all so new to him; he wasn't sure where to look. There was so much clutter, so much indecipherable white noise between him and his answer. Was this rage? He had heard rage was loud and red but he could see no new color, and heard only the white noise. With each passing breath the static grew louder and as he looked again to his boss, to his structure, to his god, suddenly it was in front of him. The static of blurred memories and voices and laughter and terror congealed into a cacophonous tone and the tiny seed of anger exploded into one clear, frozen image: the numbers. The numbers had no agenda, no history, no religion. The numbers, as they always had, told him what was and what could be, and forever what should be and the numbers told him here and forevermore that these men must live. Yet across from him this human, this imperfect, haphazard, casual growth of cells, ever evolving and ever improving millennia after millennia through nature's doing, not his own- sure evidence of his current imperfection- dared to impose his qualitative judgment over numbers. This accidental lump of temporary life dared to express providence over numbers, he thought. Deichmann scolded himself for worshipping the wrong god for so long.

"Doctor," Cadbury broke in. "If what you say is true, we have sentenced an innocent man to die."

Deichmann felt a shudder of hope. Had he misjudged the fat old man with the dead eyes?

"Better safe than sorry," said Fuller. "Let God sort 'em out."

"We're not animals, man," muttered Cadbury. "He's one of us. And he's out there just days away from certain death."

"Well, not certain death, sir," blurted Deichmann. "With their ever-increasing abilities…"

"No," interrupted Cadbury. "It's certain. If the Mukhabarat don't finish the job, our F-16's will."

"Sir?" Deichmann choked out the word.

"We've been meaning to blow up the compound for a month or two, but with the holidays and all…" He nodded to Fuller. "Bring the straight one back."

The pristine, perfect, life-giving numbers exploded in front of Deichmann's eyes in a fiery blaze, and he sank into his seat, exhausted, spent, dead.

Chapter 18

Cruz marveled at the raw power being exhibited by the man in front of him. Brooklyn's smooth, carved calves propelled him up the side of the mountain, through the snagging terrain as swiftly as a wolf, even with the old man flung limp across his shoulders. For his own part, Cruz carried both his sack and Brooklyn's, and bounded along just fine. In front of him the men were staggered fifteen to twenty meters apart, packs, guns, communications and survival equipment loaded onto their backs, vaulting toward the first plateau without so much as a strained breath. He had never been fat, never been slow, never been stupid, in fact he had never been much of anything, good or bad. He had been Cruz, Chico, Papi, the nice guy, first to smile, first to laugh. He was a decent older brother and decent younger brother and a decent uncle, because he showed up. That was his contribution and as far as he could see, that was fine. What he lacked in vision he offset with presence.

Without the military, he often wondered, where would he be? Flipping burgers with his sister, he knew, or hauling sod with the rest of the Mexican men in his neighborhood- all fine, all paid, often steady work in the affluent and stable areas of Dallas, Texas. That was and always would be his world, and that was fine, he thought.

He felt his own calves explode as he fought to keep up. He was pleasantly surprised to see the distance between him and Brooklyn hold. It was not his nature to fight, to push, but it felt good. It was also terrifying. In his neighborhood, like so many blue-collar neighborhoods, you remained loyal by remaining. Loyalty was a lack of ambition, a lack of aspiration. He watched his friends turn on those who left for college, or for menial jobs managing other Mexicans, with cold sendoffs or none at all. It wasn't until the ambitious returned in defeat that they were welcome back, and even then they were expected to make reparations, to drop in the pecking order, to apologize for the insult of desiring more than the rest had. So each wonderful, deep, grasping breath invigorated him with crisp, pure oxygen and suffocated him with guilt at the same time.

For the moment, at least, he refused to think about the greatest change of them all. In fact, he refused to believe it, at least not completely. He knew little about the gay people, but as far as he knew one could be a fag and still be straight. One could be a little gay. One could dabble, or go through a phase, which was dangerous enough. Like any tightly-woven community, that which is different is marked, and marked by all, and forever. He often heard whispers as a kid, about this guy or that guy, always in the form of warnings. You hang with so-and-so? You know he smokes pole, right? That was the kiss of death, the end for so-and-so. To be seen with so-and-so was then social suicide, you were a pole smoker by association, branded for life. Men jumped you, women ignored you, and the indifferent shrugs of the elders who witnessed everything from their porch or their open window codified the system.

It was going to be hard enough to return with stories set in worlds beyond the neighborhood, Cruz thought, and a physique. What place was there in the system for a fit, cultured pole smoker, he wondered. It never occurred to Cruz that perhaps there were other systems around the corner, that perhaps his system, his neighborhood was an immigrant holdover from the old country- an insular rural community in Mexico turned insular labor community in America, with the same superstitions, the same traps and hierarchies. Aside from stints at a handful of military bases he had lived and worked and played in a twenty square-mile radius all his short life, and like so many people whose youth is contained and circular, upon escape, he could think only of slipping back inside the system, where he could spend the remainder of his life in the relative comfort of the familiar.

That was before. But, now... Now he knew the further he ran up the mountain, the further he ran from his neighborhood, the longer it would take to return, but the less he would need to. He was breaking free, and it was terrifying.

Stirrups embraced his changes with unfailingly open arms. In a way, he had been waiting for this. Something had always felt a little off in his previous life. His body was never fully aligned, he thought. As he walked the streets or sat in a movie theater, or a mess hall, there was always something urging him to shift, to tighten, to walk out and reenter, to try again, to get it right. He believed it was a sense of purpose, something pulling him toward a new career, maybe. Perhaps it still was. Or, perhaps it was this, right now, he thought as he bolted up the mountain. It was something. Could a subconscious have a sense of destiny? Of course, he reasoned. What is a destiny, if not the achievement of one's greatest potential? The unarticulated knowledge of which lived deep inside one's own mind, he decided. Destiny was certainly not some preordained gift left for us by some divine maker to discover, or stumble upon. He was never a religious man. He would describe himself as spiritual but that meant something completely different to most people. To him, it was a sense of awe toward the universe, toward floating bodies of gas and dust that somehow found order long enough for us to traipse around and make asses of ourselves and ruin it all. That was Stirrups' understanding of the divine- it was there in form and space and structure, and it was completely, utterly incapable of interest in him or anyone else for that matter. This left him with little comfort in matters of health and safety, for instance. He found himself quite depressed when his estranged father died some years back. He was able to take no irrational comfort from friends (or strangers) who claimed that a god took his father for a reason. But his understanding of true divinity, the proven kind, the mystical gift of a temporary existence on a floating, flying star also freed him: if so many people were so wrong, so consistently about this most fundamental question of why and how, what else were they wrong about? What his superiors dismissed as wiseass remarks from a punk were really the outpourings of this cynicism toward any prevailing wisdom. Admittedly, he thought, perhaps the military was a poor choice given his proclivity for questioning authority, but is there no place in the armed forces for those who ask why? For those who question? Well, he laughed, he would certainly find out now. So many questions would be answered upon their return.

"Continue straight?" called one of the men from below.

"Never straight, always forward!" called Stirrups. It spilled out of him, a quick thoughtless reaction, and he reveled in the silliness of the statement. As he pounded his way up the trail he could hear his brothers toss the chant back and forth with varying levels of jollity. He heard them say it over and over again, with a new bent each time, stressing never, then straight, and so on, as if each new series of inflections gave it entirely new meaning. It was the first sentiment, he realized, that the entire platoon shared, certainly the first laugh. He couldn't know what it meant to each man, to call out to each other and the stars, *never straight, always forward!* He wasn't even sure this was real to him and he was by far the most comfortable, how could he know just what it meant to the others? A question for another time, he thought, answers would come. So many answers would come upon their return. For now, let them laugh and run, let them explore the words on their own.

"Never straight! Always forward!" shouted someone above. "Never straight, always forward!"

*

Newman stretched upward toward the crystalline night sky and felt the blood surge toward his aching nose. Was it broken again, or had it never healed? Who knows. Who cares. He remembered the elder, hooded and hooked to electrodes, and then a skirmish, and then… nothing. "Where are we?" he asked to no one in particular. The last few hours had passed as a bumpy, nauseating blur. He knew one thing for sure; he was no longer in charge. He had failed, and failed spectacularly.

For a moment down there he had actually believed. He had felt the adrenaline course through his twisted veins, the rush that every bully feels when he towers over his whimpering prey, and he had felt the absolute sincere conviction that his menacing, maniacal act would in some way help his boys, and his country. He thought he was Patton, and he fought like Patton, and he came undone like Patton and now he sat alone like Patton, and he knew he deserved it. It was over.

He cursed himself for not knowing his place in the world, for not admitting he was so far over the hill he wasn't welcome on the hill anymore. At least now that it was over he could be himself again, he hoped. His head remained foggy and his vision blurred, but a thrice-broken nose will do that to a man, he reasoned.

Deadweight passed carrying a small boulder that must've weighed a half-ton and set it a few meters past Newman, to fortify their current position. Richards squatted behind it and looked through a pair of night vision goggles back toward Zhakoudahouk. He could make out a small camp some ten kilometers below. The village mob had grown weary and set their camels loose to graze, the sure sign they had no intention of continuing after the platoon tonight. There was something almost quaint in their adherence to form, thought Richards, and he reflected on how much he would like to know them, to trek with them for a week or a month, to eat their food, to hear their stories. They were exotic and sincere, backwards and simple, strong in numbers and loyalty. They were fascinating to this kid from the suburbs of Nowhere, U.S.A.

The young soldier- now a general by Newman's default- lowered the night vision scopes but continued staring at the distant camp below. Newman watched the kid think for a quiet, proud moment.

"Richards?"

The boy snapped out of his distant dream and turned to Newman. "Ginger."

"How did you boys get me up here?"

"We carried you."

"You were running?"

"Yes, sir."

Newman bristled at the false invocation of a chain of command, at the obligation of it all. He wanted to be called an asshole, he wanted to be called a scumbag, a worthless piece of shit who couldn't lead a Girl Scout troop; he wanted to be told the truth. But the military and its rules, and its expectations, the absurdity of it all... He couldn't blame the kid, only himself. They both knew it was horseshit, but they would ride it out like good soldiers.

"You wouldn't lie to me, would you, Richards?"

"No, sir. Never."

Lincoln thumped down next to him. "General Ginger, SatComm for you."

"What fresh hell awaits," mumbled Newman as much to himself as to Lincoln.

Newman took the clunky phone and caught the glances of every man in the platoon. This was the first call from Kuwait since they launched. Command could have no way of knowing of his massive failure, but platoon certainly did. Newman extended the receiver to Richards.

"Take it. You're the C.O., and you know it."

"They want you, Ginger," interrupted Lincoln. "You're going home."

Newman slowly brought the phone to his ear, as if for the first time in his life. "This is Ginger," he whispered. "Yes, sir. Yes, sir. I told you that two fucking weeks ago! Yes, sir. Thank you, sir."

The men were silent. They had filled in the blanks.

"Well?" asked Richards.

"They're bringing me home."

"I guess you got your wish."

"I never wished for this."

"That's right," said Richards. "You wanted to be a hero, not a fag."

The thumping of helicopter blades grew close.

"I tried," said Newman. It was all he could muster. "I tried."

"I think I hear your ride."

Richards stalked off and the men followed. As the Huey approached it dropped from the sky like some alien aircraft, its tail swaying with the currents of air that rolled up the mountain. A rope ladder dropped in front of Newman and he grabbed it.

"Godspeed!" he called to the men. The earth seemed to rattle beneath him and he could barely make them out through the dust. Were they even looking, he wondered? But before he could steal a second glance he was being pulled into the air and onto the deck of the Huey, and suddenly into the ether of an empty night sky.

Richards gathered the men amidst the settling dust. He was no more at ease than the last time he had corralled them, but he was hurt, and he was beat, and the exhaustion swirled through him and through the fear and through the doubt and turned it all into something resembling courage, and if he didn't say something, nobody would. Well, he thought, Stirrups might say something, but he could be a bitter pill to swallow, and the men didn't need that right now.

"Boys," he began, without a clue where to go from there. He glanced at the ground, bartering for a moment to catch his thoughts. He wished someone would tell him what to say, tell him what the men wanted to hear or needed to hear. It occurred to him that it was now his job to know these things, to lead without being led. He expected a wave of panic and a thousand little voices inside his head screaming "run!", but they never came. Only one voice came crashing through the nerves and the doubt, and it was his. It was his by Newman Ginger's default, but it had to be his, and so it was. He was a soldier, after all.

"Boys, I don't know what to say." He noticed some of the men shift uncomfortably, rightly wondering if he was up to this. "If I'm being completely honest, we're better off. I'm sad for the old man, but we're better off, and that's a good thing, because we have one hell of a fight ahead." This seemed to pique their interest, which startled Richards. They were not scared. They actually wanted to be challenged, and to be told the truth, he thought. "The enemy is strong, and swift, and disciplined, we know that. But so are we. We can win." He noticed a few heads nod. This was good, he knew. "We can win," he repeated. This time he meant it.

Chapter 19

As CentCom came into view from the chopper Newman noticed the fortified walls, doubled-up and ringed with barbed wire, and the masked, shaded watch towers, and the squat, square buildings the color of sand whose bunkers must extend deep into the earth, and the satellite dishes that dotted the roofs of each, and the camouflaged trucks that darted in and out of every entrance. From this height it looked like some prehistoric sea monster dotted with venomous pores, shitting its blood onto the sand in its beached death throes, miles from the sea.

As bleak as CentCom looked, he was nevertheless grateful to get out of this gyrating, airborne coffin. He had already thrown up, twice, in the long trek from Northern Iraq to Kuwait, and the deckhands who initially regarded him as a mess with his broken nose, and disheveled, sweat and dirt-soaked appearance were outright horrified now, and openly mocked him. He wrapped himself deeper into the fire blanket they provided and shrunk into the bucket seat, counting the minutes until this winged nightmare touched down.

As the chopper lowered toward the tarmac Newman began to see signs of life, of the crisp, whip-smart movement of the men and women. This cumbersome clump of stone and wire and steel had an elegant inner life, and he was suddenly intimidated not by the size but by the sophistication of it all. Trucks and carts zipped from point to point, shepherded by armed men and women, and street lights and makeshift roads carved paths through the chunky, low buildings, and a fleet of Hueys and Blackhawks were maintained and serviced in broad strokes of manpower. It was a living, breathing city system, half man and half machine.

They touched down and were instantly folded into the system. Without a word the deckhands unbuckled Newman and handed him down to helmeted men, and he was whipped past more helmeted men wheeling gasoline and tools and mechanical parts toward the panting chopper, coming to rest like a spent war horse. He was thrust through double doors and whisked down a flight of stairs and down another and another and through an unmarked door and suddenly they were pushing him through a cramped hallway lit by single fluorescent bulbs, spaced meters and meters apart. One of the men let go of his arm long enough to jab open another unmarked door and the second man threw him inside.

Without a word they turned and left. Before Newman could form a thought, a squat, soft looking man appeared in the open doorway, and through the spilled fluorescent light from the hallway Newman recognized him instantly. He was on the firing range that day, during the battery of tests- not the scientist, but his minder. The small man entered the room and gave a quick tug on an invisible chain, and a single overhead bulb clicked on. In the light he could see the man's sunken eyes and red nose, and this relaxed Newman, for amidst the deadly efficiency of everyone on this base it appeared he was left in the care of a fellow washout drunk.

The man smiled at Newman, and wobbled back and forth. He was lit, thought Newman. Weary but emboldened, Newman took a small step forward. "I thought I was screaming into the wind."

"Hmph," the man grunted. "Tell me about it."

"Pardon?" asked Newman.

"What?" said the man.

"What am I doing here?" said Newman. "Do I still have a job?"

"We…" the man swallowed, trying to pin down the words before they slipped away. "We've got something for you."

"Not another experiment, I hope."

The man did not respond. He narrowed his eyes and glared at Newman. "I wanted to see you in the flesh, you know that?" The words were gummy and staggered. Newman felt his arms and legs tense. Something about the man's gaze suggested more than curiosity, something closer to fury, or disgust, and the stars on his lapel put Newman squarely at his mercy. "You don't fool me," he muttered as he slowly backed out of the room, never taking his eyes off Newman. "You don't fool me," he said again, and slammed the door shut. Newman heard the telltale click and thud of the lock and latch as they were jammed into place. He had not been rescued, he realized. He had been captured.

He dropped the fire blanket and looked around. The room appeared to be quite deep, and the only wall he could see was directly in front of him, between him and the hallway. Everything else was indistinguishable and the echoes of the drunk's voice still hung in the distant corners. A steel table flanked by a steel chair on either side sat squarely behind him, on the edge of the light, and beyond that, darkness. He would probably be interrogated here at this very table, he knew, or perhaps offered some quid pro quo that would fall somewhere between degrading and deadly. After all, this was not the V.I.P. suite.

"You deserve this, Newman," he said to himself. "You deserve this."

"Do you?" came a voice from the dark.

Newman spun around and searched for his side-arm, but it was gone. "Identify yourself!" he screamed. "Identify yourself immediately!"

A diminutive figure slowly emerged from the shadows. Newman looked to the man's hands for weapons and, finding nothing, began looking past him for muscle, but the man appeared to be alone. His white lab coat came into crisp focus and erased any fears Newman had of physical confrontation. As the man stepped to the edge of the small pool of light, Newman recognized him finally. He had been with the drunk on the testing fields, watching, monitoring. It quickly occurred to Newman that the two men who had hawked the platoon during the tests were probably intimately responsible for the platoon's fate, so this little scientist had pull. Perhaps he had been responsible for bringing

Newman to safety in Kuwait, and that made him the closest thing Newman had to an ally.

"You're the scientist?" he asked.

"You are the infamous Newman Ginger?"

"General Newman Ginger," he corrected. "Who the hell are you?"

"I am the one who convinced the powers that be that you were spared the effects of the bomb," he said. Newman's eyes widened. "Due, of course, to your broken nose."

"I've been saying that for two fucking weeks!" Newman exploded.

"Well, it's a lie," said Deichmann. "Regardless of whether you could smell the love bomb, you most certainly inhaled it. Can you imagine if smell alone dictated the efficacy of our chemical weapons," he said with a snort. "Anthrax would be rather easy to marginalize, wouldn't it?" Deichmann held two fingers to his nose, and pinched.

"You're wrong!" screamed Newman. "It didn't happen to me! It didn't happen to me!" Newman moved to his right, around the table and toward the little man, who shuffled to his right, using the metallic table as a buffer between himself and the general.

"It didn't happen to me," Deichmann mocked the old man. "It won't happen to me. It can't happen to me." He lowered his voice to a tight whisper. "It... can't... happen... to me." He drew out the words and leveled his eyes with Newman's.

Newman stopped chasing him, reached for the chair in front of him, and sat.

"What happened to me?" Newman's voice trailed off as his mind sprinted back to that dawn, to the river, to the canisters streaking across the sky trailing their purple gas. Then the thud, and black. Blood everywhere. Standing in the river, purple haze swirling about. His nose was broken, he knew, but his mouth and lungs were not. If he could breathe, he breathed that gas. He recalled it now, but he had known it then.

"What happened to me?" he asked again.

"I happened to you, general," began Deichmann. "I created a stimulant that looses man of all inhibitions, thereby releasing him to become himself. His true self."

"But the muscles," stammered Newman, "and the speed, and the courage…"

"We are greater than we could ever know, general. Our true self is our best self, and we possess- buried beneath fear, and lies, and religion and sadness-" He paused not for effect, but to ensure the general's understanding. "Beneath those enslaving layers of inhumanity, we possess greatness, general. You and your men have only begun to scratch the surface."

"My men…" mumbled Newman. His head felt light upon his shoulders and he gripped the underside of the table to steady himself out of the scientist's view.

"Your men are bigger, stronger, faster, with an increased sense of purpose and drive," shouted Deichmann. "All thanks to me!"

Newman sensed a shift in the little man. There was a hysterical quality to his tone now, as if Newman was arguing each point with him. "You and your men are a gift to the United States military from me, its humble servant. We now have the power, general, to turn the entire country into the greatest fighting force this world has ever seen, an army so physically and mentally superior we could secure our borders, ensure democracy and freedom, and peace, general, peace throughout the entire world, simply by turning the entire country…"

"Gay?" said Newman.

"Gay."

"It would be the end of procreation..."

"But not fertilization."

"…the end of marriage..."

"But not love."

"…the end of the natural order…"

"In the wrong hands!" barked Deichmann. "But the threat alone would ensure foreign powers bend to our whims, kneel before us…" He shook with excitement. "You see, there is no need to actually activate a second Love Bomb, general. Your platoon is my Hiroshima!"

"What?" whispered Newman.

"You are the new nuclear option, general."

"So it's over," said Newman. "You have your test case, you can show us off to the world..."

"…unless Cadbury has his way."

"What do you mean?"

"You must save your platoon, general."

"Save them from what?"

"Isn't it obvious? Those men are never coming back." Deichmann slid a thin dossier across the table. It was open to the final page- launch codes and coordinates overlaid on a topographical map of some mountainous terrain. Newman had seen these coordinates before, over an identical topo map of northern Iraq, the one handed to him by his trusted friend and colleague, General Fuller on the eve of the mission. The topo map that he was handed originally, however, had no launch codes, for the platoon had no missiles. These codes were a clear directive for Air Force pilots to bomb the exact same Iraqi hangars that the platoon was hoofing toward at this very moment.

"What is this?" asked Newman, refusing to admit what he already knew. The doctor, to his credit, did not answer, did not rob Newman of the painful but crucial moment where fear evolves into truth. "They're going to bomb the platoon?"

"The second they reach the Mukhabarat."

"They wouldn't do that! They'd kill the special ops we were sent to…" His voice left him. There were no special ops. It was a suicide mission. They had been sent to slaughter.

"No one is safe, Newman. The second your platoon is gone, Burnam will be next to go."

Newman recalled the drunk in the doorway and knew he was Burnam, a man certainly on his way out. Deichmann continued, "A heart attack, a fishing accident. Then Fuller. His rank can't protect him, he knows too much. He'll catch some obscure desert flu. Maybe his chopper will hit an untimely sandstorm." Newman, to his own surprise, was ambivalent. Perhaps he understood Fuller's role in this more than he was willing to admit.

"And you?" he asked.

"Me?" the little man repeated, as if his own fate was of so little consequence he had not yet considered the mortal danger he was in. "I suppose this is the last time you'll ever see me, general," he said, allowing a calculated note of melancholy to slip through. "My legacy is slated to die in the hills of northern Iraq."

He watched the old man disappear into his thoughts for a few moments. Though this Newman was unremarkable, he was a general, Deichmann thought. He had gone through training, and war, and service, and life. He had experienced physical and mental challenges that Deichmann could hardly fathom, and though he had slowly rotted over the decades, there was reason to hope that this once strong man could find his power again. After all, he was hit with the bomb and it was empirically impossible that he could have somehow nullified the world-altering effects of Deichmann's gas. But to look at him, what signs of greatness had emerged over the ensuing weeks?

Deichmann studied the yellowing bruises around the old man's eyes and nose, and the wild flock of hair, and the caked sweat and dirt, and most discouragingly, the sad, dead eyes. Had the bomb reached him too late in life, Deichmann wondered, an electric shock of panic streaking through his body. Was it possible that the frontal cortex had somehow hardened or formed its own protective shell to lock a man into his own mediocrity at a certain age? No, he thought. Absolutely not. I refuse to believe that, he thought. We are all capable of greatness, he insisted to himself, again, as he had done so many times in the development of the bomb. He looked at Newman again. He had chosen this man because it was his only shot, he was the only member of the platoon who could be smuggled past the neanderthals in charge, and he therefore must be sufficient. Deichmann knew he had mere hours left on this earth, and he must bequeath the bomb's legacy to General Newman Ginger once and for all, or take it to the grave, and though the old, washed up general did not exactly inspire confidence, he was here, and he was listening, and that would have to be enough. There was simply no other choice.

Newman finally broke the silence. "Doctor, there is one thing I don't understand. If the potion was designed simply to release the real man that lies locked inside each of us, how could you be sure that we would all turn out… gay?"

Deichmann smiled. "General, aren't we all at least a little gay?"

He set a small figurine of the Virgin Mary cradling the baby Jesus on the steel table between them. "Take this, and keep it safe."

Newman picked up the figurine. He always considered himself a deeply religious man, but the naked weirdness of the moment overtook any piousness the doctor may have wanted him to experience. "What do I do with this?" he asked.

"When the journey seems bleakest," he began.

"What journey," interrupted Newman.

"When all seems lost…"

"What journey are you referring to..."

"Pull her out, and ask her guidance..."

"Are you listening to me," cried Newman. "What..."

"She contains your salvation, General Ginger," he said as he stood and moved into the shadows again. "Call upon her in your time of need and she will replenish you."

Newman listened as the doctor's footsteps drifted into the dark. Without thinking he stood and followed, quickly tucking the figurine into one of the many cargo pockets on his uniform. He held his hands out in front of him to protect himself, and he could hear the echo of his footsteps rising in pitch as he approached the wall. Suddenly he was there, the cold stone against his hands. He followed it to his right, but the doctor's footsteps were gone. He slid further and further along the wall, into the abyss. He looked back and the interrogation table with its single overhead bulb was gone. Had the room curved, or dipped? He remembered a flight instructor once described the sensation of remaining level while his plane banked 40 degrees through a cloud covered night into an ever-tightening spiral- without the visual cues of a horizon he was lost and banked in downward circles toward his death, the centrifugal forces pulling him down and in faster and faster as he went. If it wasn't for a momentary break in the clouds he would never have seen the jagged, dutched lines of the cityscape screaming toward him only a few seconds before the trajectory and velocity of his twin-engine locked him into the death spiral. The pilot yanked the little bird back to level, and credited that sliver of crooked light for saving his life. Newman pulled the tiny flashlight from the canvas pouch on his belt and flicked it on. Ahead of him the concrete floor clearly dipped and disappeared around a corner. He turned and aimed the thin beam behind him and saw the floor shoot up and level off thirty meters back, at the top of what he now realized was a ramp. He noticed the heavy cement door, a meter thick, open at the top of the ramp. It was laden with latches and bolts and made to look like any other segment of cement wall- a trap door for secret entrances and exits, used to spook prisoners as it allowed interrogators to come and go in silence, as if materializing suddenly out of the ether. It struck him that he was now, officially, an escaped prisoner. He angled the flashlight to the landing below, steeled himself and continued into the bowels of Cent-Com, Kuwait.

He was convinced he heard a second set of foot-steps ahead. He quickened his pace, the flashlight in his right hand and his left running along the pockmarked concrete. At the fourth landing he was certain he heard the click-clack of the doctor's soles against the concrete and he ran toward the sound. As he circled the fifth landing he saw a sliver of light ahead, shrinking away from him. He lowered his flashlight and sprinted to-ward it. The light was collapsing but he could make out the end of the concrete wall and the beginning of a closing door and he leapt forward and jammed his tiny flashlight into the partition. It held long enough for him to wedge his fingers into the gap and tug against the pressurized seal. To his astonishment the door held, and then without warning, swung itself open in a smooth, steady arc, as if guided by some pressurized arm. Light poured in and Newman shielded his eyes as he stepped out of the hidden passageway and into a simple, sterile hallway. He looked to his right and saw the tail of the doctor's lab coat, a white flash at the end of the hallway. He sprinted down the corridor and burst into the perpendicular hallway only to find him-self in the Central Command, perched on an overlook, peering down into a massive theater of monitors, chirp-ing screens and control booths, manned by uniformed intelligence operatives bouncing from station to station. No one noticed him, in large part because their atten-tion seemed glued to the three-story monitor plastered to the far wall, displaying real time intelligence pouring in from around the Middle East. Newman scanned the monitor from right to left and guessed its width at some two hundred feet.

A commotion broke out to his left along the overlook. It was the doctor, and he thrashed against the grip of two uniformed guards. Newman stood stone still and reminded himself to breathe. He was still a uniformed general as far as anyone here knew. Without warning one of the guards jabbed something into the doctor's ribs and the little man crumpled into the second guard's arms.

As they whisked the doctor away, Newman watched the little man disappear and found himself... ambivalent. He had endured a wretched couple of weeks because of that man and his insane ideas and designs. Nothing made sense anymore, nothing seemed to fit. There was a life, and a routine, and a system and it used to be Newman's, and it used to be clean, and clear. It wasn't special, or significant, or meaningful, or revolutionary in any way, but it was his. That little son of a bitch- and his superiors- had swooped in and changed everything. They had used him as a lab rat, he thought, and now it was fine, fair even, that the doctor should endure some radical interference with his life as he knew it, as Newman was sure he would. But, on the other hand, he thought, the doctor brought him back. The doctor had also intervened and led Newman from that dungeon, at his peril. If there had been no humanity, no true concern, he wouldn't be standing here right now, he thought.

Newman looked across the pit of monitors and lights and agents scuttling around. Doing their best, he thought. At the beck and call of their masters, he knew. He saw, for the first time, the real strata of the service.

It wasn't a dozen levels of experience and pay grades, it was the hustling, scrapping, fighting men and women on the ground with their hands in the muck, and the tiny, distant masters they served. He saw his boys in the mountains, clawing through brush and sand to rescue… ghosts. Serving their masters, walking straight off a cliff.

He ran toward the spot where the doctor had been abducted and saw just ahead a small plaque affixed to a double glass door, "Secretary of Defense, William Cadbury". The little bastard had led him to the very top. He pushed the doors open and stepped in, and to his astonishment, Cadbury's three assistants betrayed no signs of surprise. They quietly ceased typing, and filing, and dialing and looked to Newman.

"The Secretary will see you now, General Ginger," said one.

Newman was frozen. Had he heard her correctly? His eyes darted around the room. "You seem agitated, sir," she continued. "Can I bring you some water?"

"The secretary will see you now, General Ginger," repeated another, standing.

Newman felt himself slip through the room though he was certain his feet were encased in concrete. In a breath he was inside the office of the most powerful warlord on planet earth, the Secretary of Defense of the United States of America. Not since God has one being had so much influence to shape the world. Tectonic plates were shifted from this office, at the whims of this single man. What a tremendous burden, thought Newman, to own the future.

Cadbury spun around in his chair to see the general, The One. Perhaps he had avoided the bomb, thought

Cadbury, but he hadn't escaped unscathed. He was a mess, standing there shaking and sweat-soaked. He hadn't shaved in days, Cadbury thought. Remind me again why we saved this buffoon? But we did, we did. We brought him back, and we owe him an explanation, and he owes the United States an ironclad vow of silence. The only living men who knew of the events of the last two weeks were in the room at this very moment, save for Fuller and Howell, two unimpeachable loyalists. There were no witnesses left, aside from the walking dead up on that mountain, Cadbury thought, so let's get on with it and bring the old man around. His dossier pegged Newman as a god-fearing man, a believer and a loyalist, so this should be easy.

Newman watched the Secretary study him with cold, tiny eyes. He recalled the man's public pronouncements on the holiness of missions the United States had undertaken in various countries over the years and he found a small measure of hope in the man's public piousness. He would appeal to that, to the highest calls for love and charity and life, he thought. He would appeal to the man's Christian decency.

"General Ginger," said Cadbury. "Thank you for coming to see me."

"Thank you?" said Newman. "Thank you, of course. Thank you for bringing me in."

"Have a seat."

"I was not expecting…" began Newman, but his voice failed him as he sat across from the secretary.

"Let me guess," said Cadbury. "The scientist found you, and he spooked you. He told you you were not safe, yes?"

"Well, no sir. The cell I was placed in told me I was not safe."

"Oh my, I'm so sorry," said Cadbury. His eyes narrowed to dead, black slits at Newman's arrogance. Did he not see the blade inches from his soiled neck? "I assure you, General, no harm will come, and no offense was intended."

"Is it true, sir?"

"Is what true, General?"

"The doctor, the scientist… He came to me with certain information."

"Coordinates?" asked Cadbury. "Classified orders of a bombing run?"

Newman paused. He knew better than to answer, it was not a question.

"You were brought here- you were allowed here- for one reason," said Cadbury.

"Yes, sir?"

"I needed to see you myself. I needed to look into your eyes, and ask you a question, and hear your response for myself before making a final decision about your… fitness."

"My fitness, sir?"

"Are you a god-fearing man, Ginger?"

"Pardon, sir?"

"Do you read the good book?"

"I have, sir. Yes."

"Are you familiar with Romans?"

"Not off the top of my head, sir."

"Revelatur enim ira Dei," he began, rolling each word out with the weight and hue of solid gold. "De caelo super omnem impietatem." He locked eyes with Newman. "The wrath of God will be revealed from

Heaven, against all ungodliness. Is it any wonder this chapter is titled Romans? The most advanced civilization in the world was not built in a day, but it burned to the ground in mere hours. Do you know why, general?"

"Hubris, sir? War?"

"Eroticism, general."

"Pardon, sir?"

"Eroticism. The culture of indulgence. Homosexuals."

Newman shuddered and reflexively brought his hand to his neck.

"Rome was the gayest country the world has ever known," continued Cadbury. "Where is it now? Gone. Ashes. Dust."

Newman was almost certain that Rome still existed, but he was not about to argue the point.

"Your platoon is an affront to God, General Ginger," said Cadbury. "The United States military may be the greatest fighting force the world has ever known, but there is one general we do not want to face."

"My god," said Ginger, at once horrified and confused.

"Exactly," said Cadbury.

"You're psychotic," he blurted out. He stood and backed toward the door. "With all due respect, Mister Secretary, you've lost your mind."

"If you think for one second I'm going to be the Secretary of Defense who presided over the summoning of God's wrath upon the United States of America, you are the psychotic, General Ginger! Harkening the Rapture upon us would be the very antithesis of my role here in the Defense Department!"

Newman backed through the doors and ran through the anteroom. The secretaries were gone, papers mysteriously deserted next to printers, a phone off its base, the dial tone spilling out and filling the room. He could hear Cadbury call after him, "Run, you coward! Run back to your godless sodomites!" He was dizzy and certain he was quickly going blind. The colors of hallway after hallway swirled into a blinding white and he led himself forward only by the handrail drilled into the walls. He tumbled into corners as he overshot the sharp turn at the end of each hallway, where it doubled back on itself just before ramping upward at impossible inclines. He tripped over his own feet and his legs became heavy and thick with exhaustion. He pulled himself up and pushed ahead blindly until a sudden and familiar sound filtered through the interminable walls: wind. He dragged one leg and then the next toward the wisp of rich, life-giving wind and he could feel it now, it grew stronger and stronger as if to blow him back down into the cancerous pit of Central Command. He pushed forward and slowly the white of the world was overtaken by yellows and browns and then his hand was on glass. He punched at the middle of the door and found more glass, then moved his hand down toward his waist and there it was. He punched low and swift and the handle gave and the door swung open into the wind. Newman staggered forward and collapsed into the sand, and rolled onto his back. The world was boiling and he inhaled deeply, sucking in the elements. The entire world was upside down now, but behind him he could make out the fortified edges of the compound, in front of him only vacillating heat waves obscuring the endless desert. He was outside the walls of CentCom. He was free.

A low rumble broke the even howl of the desert wind. Something was tearing along the ceiling of the world toward him, toward his head, right now. He rolled onto his stomach and struggled to his knees as the black town car barreled toward him. It swung wide and cut in from of him, forming a curtain of sand and dirt. He could barely see the doors swing open. Two operatives in black suits, black ties and black sunglasses marched toward him. Newman backpedaled until he slammed into the perimeter of CentCom. Newman knew these men, their corps. These were the men you called when you needed something or someone to disappear. They were unidentifiable and interchangeable, masters of the darkest arts. They operated outside of any jurisdiction because they didn't exist, and if they came for you, you no longer existed.

"General Newman Ginger," said one.

"Get in," said the other.

They took his arms above the elbow and threw him through an open rear door. Before he could blink they were seated on both sides of him and the car knifed into the vast Kuwaiti desert.

"How are you feeling, general?" asked one of the agents.

"Where are you taking me?"

"The Secretary has asked us to offer you an opportunity, general."

"We want you to press the red button, Newman."

"The red button?"

"You've always been a good soldier, haven't you, Ginger?"

"Not really," he blurted out. "Have you seen my record?"

"You wouldn't want the secretary to have his fingerprints all over this, would you Newman?"

"It wouldn't look very kosher."

"It wouldn't look very kosher, Newman."

"The secretary is a respected man, a good Christian."

"But, on the other hand, if this bombing run originated from an overzealous general…"

"A washout…"

"A man in over his head…"

"Wait just one second," said Newman. "You want me to… " He looked to the man on either side but their stone jaws were set and revealed nothing. "No! I won't! These are good boys, they deserve a chance!"

"There will be in investigation."

"You will be cleared of any dereliction, Newman."

"You may even earn yourself that second star, General."

"A promotion?" cried Newman. "Oh, no! I know how you people operate. You'll get rid of me, just like you got rid of that drunk, Burnam!"

"And Deichmann," said one of the agents, through the slightest a smile.

"You're sick! All of you! I won't do it! I won't!"

"The secretary will be sorry to hear that."

"Thank you for your service, General." The agents flung open the rear doors and leapt from the speeding car without a word. Newman perched on the back seat to look through the rear window. The agents rolled three and four times through the sand, sprung to their feet and instantly a second town car was upon them, rear doors open. They threw themselves into the back-seats and Newman watched as the car spun and sped away, disappearing into the torrents of sand and dirt that followed everything here in this sweltering purgatory.

He sunk into his seat and released every muscle in his body. He let each bump in the road pummel him from below, and the upward shock of each bounced him like a limp rag doll. Pain shot through his spine and neck as evermore-awkward positions jammed vertebrae against vertebrae. The car seemed to speed up. He heard fireworks, then a symphony. As his eyes closed, he caught the slightest tilt of the driver's head, his black sunglasses now angled into the rearview mirror. This young, sturdy agent of devastation appeared to be intrigued by the flailing clump of weathered bone and tissue in the back seat. Newman wondered what was whipping round and round and up the tiny plastic coil that led to the man's earpiece: probably instructions on exactly how to dispose of his body. He collapsed onto the seat like he had so many nights onto his own bed, drunk on fine rye, a military history in his hands, awe and jealousy equal in his heart, in love with his army and ashamed of his uselessness. What will come, will come, he thought. But, if he was going to die today, he was at least going to be comfortable.

Chapter 20

Cadbury was so incensed by his exchange with the old man he allowed the aides to lead him to one of the armored elevators outside his office instead of heading for the ramped hallways he swore by. He stared straight ahead as it plunged into the earth, a hundred meters below the central command of Central Command. He expected to feel the epileptic rush he had come to crave from his years marching down the ramps, but this god forsaken electric box had robbed him of the slow and steady charge of oil energy, and the elevator swiftly stopped and the stainless steel doors drew open.

They stood in front of a supply closet and a card was produced and swiped along the crease between the closet door and the frame. Two successive chirps and the door slid into the wall. Cadbury and the young aides marched into the second and final command center at CentCom, the only one that counted: the consecrated War Room, a sharply focused command center for active and volatile missions. Where the grownups come to play, thought Cadbury.

Uniformed, decorated men strode through the aisles and muttered single-word commands to rows and rows of computer jockeys attached to sophisticated command systems. Screens blanketed the walls, maps and live-feeds rear-projected onto them. Cadbury was led to a quiet, dark corner, a command station with its own monitors for isolated, classified directives.

"What are we looking at?" he snarled at the command engineer, seated in front of a bank of monitors, keyboards, and joysticks.

"Sir, this is a specially positioned satellite system tracking the gay platoon," said the engineer. He pointed out six pulsing, pink dots on top of a digital topographic map. "It's essentially a form of radar established specifically for tracking the gay platoon."

"Gay radar?"

"Yes, sir. Gay radar." He waited to gauge the secretary's reaction but Cadbury stared blankly back at him, waiting for further explanation. "And, and…" he stammered, "I've come up with a shorthand for this new system, something concise and catchy." He waited for approval to continue, some sign that the secretary had even the most remote interest in this exciting new technology and its branding.

"Go on!" Cadbury finally barked.

"I call it 'Gay-Dar', sir." He beamed like a proud father.

His desperation was sickening to Cadbury. What in the flaming hell was this peon so giddy about? He ought to be demoted on principle, thought Cadbury.

"It'll never stick," said Cadbury, with a wave. "Send it to Acronyms and Abbreviations, let the professionals handle this."

"Yes, sir," choked the engineer. He knew Acronyms and Abbreviations was good for only two things:

terrifically terrible acronyms and abbreviations, and the snail-like pace at which they worked, testing every possible combination of words, letters, hyphenates and punctuation with focus group after focus group after focus group... By the time they were done, if they ever finished, his deliciously simple and precise software would receive some painfully generic title, of little or no relation to its form or function, something designed to hammer any of the joy and charm out, to turn its vibrant colors grey, to squeeze and process and bludgeon it into the most bland, palatable form imaginable, offensive to no one, attractive to no one. He had often overheard superiors bitch about the dearth of creativity that their men and women exhibited. He had taken it as a call to action, he had invented and coined Gay-Dar, and within seconds of its unveiling, it was dead. Too unique, too bold, too fresh… Too creative, he sniped to himself. In some small way, he thought, this was a relief: the dearth of creativity was not some failing on the part of the soldiers, it was not his failure, but a crippling kink built into the system, a ceiling bolted onto the cage in which they were all trapped, paid for by the men with the money, with the say-so, with the power. Hey, he thought. Fuck 'em. I tried.

"What are those little brown dots, a few miles south of the platoon?" asked Cadbury.

"Those are the villagers, sir."

"Our boys are being chased?"

"It appears that way, sir."

"Interesting," said Cadbury. He released the hint of a smile.

"Our boys have created significant separation in an astonishingly short period of time," said the engineer, hopeful that this bit of good news would re-ingratiate him, but Cadbury's smile disappeared.

"Sir," asked an aide, "suppose the platoon hunkers down in those mountains. Couldn't they, theoretically, survive indefinitely?"

"Not if we cut off their food supply," said Cadbury.

The engineer knew better than to acknowledge the seemingly backwards objective implied by this statement. He shifted in his seat, hoping to find a position that suggested he was both not listening and at attention.

"But," said the second aide, "suppose they reach CentCom with an urgent S.O.S. Wouldn't the PointCom, theoretically, be obligated to ensure an emergency delivery, or other support, as requested?"

"Good point," said Cadbury. "Cut off all satellite communications."

"Yes, sir," said the aides in concert.

The engineer pretended to type something on one of his keyboards and then another. He prayed that he looked busy enough to appear nonplussed by the command to abandon the tiny, gay platoon in hostile enemy territory. He caught himself typing too loudly, too conspicuously, and noticed one of the aides' gaze shift over. He pulled back and took a sip of cold coffee from a paper cup he kept topped off at all times. It was thin and bitter but it distracted him from the noose he felt slip around his neck, tightening with each second the secretary stood behind him.

Cadbury turned to him. "Follow them down on their approach. Send the birds in as soon as the first shots are fired."

The engineer choked down the last drops of coffee. "Yes, sir." He fought to keep the words steady and even. He had spoken those two words tens of thousands of times in his decade of service, but this was the first time he had to think about them first. He knew what he must say, of course, Yes, sir. He also knew what he should say, or scream, or demand. He had just witnessed a senior officer order the murder of a United States military platoon in the field. He had been ordered to initiate the attack himself.

"Gentlemen," said Cadbury, an air of wistful pride in his voice. "We are on the eve of a noble massacre. Let us pray for a swift resolution."

The engineer spun around in his chair and took the secretary's cold, leathery hand in one of his, and an aide's in the other, hung his head, and wondered just what those six men on the mountain had done to deserve this fate. He prayed for them, and then for himself.

*

Lincoln kneeled down some two hundred meters ahead of the pack. He had separated himself to earn a few moments to pull out the SatComm and place an urgent call to base out of earshot of the platoon. They were running low on food- the powdered MRE's they had stocked up on were dwindling, as was their water supply. One unfortunate and frightening side effect of their increased size and strength and stamina was increased thirst. They had rapidly become human Goliaths, and their bodies demanded huge amounts of water to stay hydrated. The sprint up the mountain drained them and their supply, and it was Lincoln's estimation that the platoon would soon reach a crisis point. He had the good sense to relay this concern to their PointCom, certain they could arrange to re-up in a matter of hours by diverting one of the supply teams in nearby Turkey, or even Kuwait, before broaching this subject with Richards or the platoon, with whom he would risk inducing a panic. The unit may be tiny in number, he reasoned, but the rescue mission was a top strategic priority and CentCom would most certainly aid the platoon with such mission-critical requests as food and water.

He depressed the power switch and held it for a three-count, and began to type the seven-digit code that would bring him into the military's secure communications network. No chirps, he thought. Where were they? He checked the power. There was juice. But no chirps. The SatComm would not connect.

Stirrups knelt next to him, first up. He pulled the scope from his pack and pointed it back down the hill, past the boys. They had continued to pull away from the villagers, now barely visible even through the high-powered scope. He knew, however, each stop allowed the camelback mob to regain precious ground.

"Let's keep moving," he said, before noticing Lincoln's ashen expression. "What is it?"

"SatComm is dead."

Stirrups felt his stomach drop. SatComm was the lifeline, the umbilical cord. In the back of his mind at all times- and surely in the back of everyone else's mind- was the knowledge that CentCom was watching, waiting, ready to send in the birds for a quick airlift the moment the SpecOps were freed, or sooner if variables arose.

Richards was next up. He noticed the boys watch him approach, and the way Lincoln held the SatComm, low and down, casually, pointlessly. He stopped.

"SatComm is dead," said Lincoln. "No signal."

"MRE's? Water?"

Lincoln shook his head.

"How are we getting out of here," he asked himself as much as anyone. The rest of the platoon arrived, Deadweight, Two Strikes and Cruz. Richards took a quick inventory: no food, no water, no ride. The mission was rapidly deteriorating. To retreat would mean a bloody confrontation with the villagers. To hunker down would mean a complete depletion of supplies. There was only move.

"We're going in early," he said. He pulled the topo map from his pack and spread it across a flat patch of rock. He pointed to a light green ring near the top of the peak. "We're here. Mission plan was to continue to climb, then drop in from here." He pointed to a dip between peaks that created a natural alley leading to the rear of the Mukhabarat hangars. It was a perfect route: easy to scout, easy to scale. "That's out, now." It would take hours to reach that alley, and they didn't have hours. They had to move now. The men shifted uncomfortably.

He found a thin but workable ridge that ran almost 360 degrees around the hangars. They would have to cut down to it from their current position. Once there, they would have to attack almost immediately, for the ridge offered little protection if they should be spotted. He ordered the men to move out, to begin the descent toward the ridge from which they would launch the surgical strike that would free those SpecOps, trapped and tortured, they had been told, for months.

Lincoln waited until the men had begun their descent, and called to Richards.

"This is a redundant system, Richards."

"So what?"

"If one satellite fails, we're instantaneously picked up by another," he said. "Signal failure never happens."

"Apparently it does, private," said Richards. He picked up his pack, slung it over his shoulder and began jogging down after his boys. "Move out, private," he called over his shoulder.

Lincoln stuffed the SatComm into his pack. He had done what he could. Leave your doubts on the mountain, he thought. It was time to follow.

*

The town car rolled to a stop and Newman opened his eyes. Even the rich tint of the windows could not dull the midday sun out here. The door flung open and Newman felt his hair and collar tugged and pulled and suddenly he was on his knees in the sand. He could hear the trunk open and metal rattle against metal. He could hear the agent upon him but it was the shovel he saw first.

"Dig," said the agent.

He used the shovel to balance as he pulled himself from his knees. He had one good swing, he knew, before the agent could respond. Anything short of killing the young man would be a death sentence. He also knew the agent would be expecting a swing at first, but perhaps if he looked defeated and broken and simply dug for a few minutes the agent would let his guard down, look away. He needed only the slightest opening.

The agent leaned against the car as he watched.

Newman dug, one eye on the agent and one on the sand. The young man was a rock. Square jaw, square shoulders, square head. 25, maybe 26 he guessed. Former military. Probably a wrestler, or a fullback. Someone with finely tuned reflexes, someone who lived for contact, for the fight.

Newman, on the other hand, was a wilted old cod with a shovel and withdrawal headaches. His arms and back throbbed with every thrust, and he would whip this large metal bludgeon around and take down this wrecking ball of a man, how, exactly? He laughed to himself. He was hopeless, exhausted. The agent had not broken his gaze once.

Newman stopped and dropped the shovel. He took off his sweat-soaked shirt and threw it on the ground.

"Let's go, old man," muttered the agent. "Dig."

Newman wondered why the young man would bother to prod him. Newman had offered no resistance in hours. He was barely alive as it was. Did the kid fear him? Or did he fear the next step in this process? Shooting a general in the United States military at point blank range was major league shit, Newman thought. Was this kid major league material?

Newman sized up the boy.

"Keep digging, asshole," growled the agent.

The answer- the answer to all of it- hit Newman square in the gut and he felt himself split again, at once in the ditch and ten feet above. This time, however, he was not scared. He was not scared.

He watched himself wipe the sweat from his forehead and place one foot on the rim of the ditch, as if to test the agent.

"You know why I'm out here?" he said. "I'm part of that program."

"Keep digging," said the agent, as he looked away. Newman let the opening come and go, and watched as he took a second step toward the agent, who immediately stiffened.

"If there's something you want, all you have to do is ask," he watched himself say.

"What?"

"I see the way you look at me." He continued toward the agent.

"Keep digging," barked the agent. He pulled his gun from its holster and held it at his side. Newman was close enough now he could reach for the gun.

"Why?" he said. "You like to watch?"

"I oughtta shoot you right now, old man."

"Then you'd have to dig," said Newman. He was inches from the young, gay man. Newman watched as he placed his hands on the agent's hips and pulled him close.

"I'm warning you, general," muttered the agent.

Newman saw himself kiss the agent. He felt the young man's spine loosen and lips part. Through the thick black sunglasses he could see the boy's eyes close and he wondered for a fleeting moment if he was the boy's first. As he made his way down, he felt a twinge of sadness that he would be the boy's last.

Newman watched himself unbuckle the agent's belt and unzip his zipper, and he saw the young man lift his face to the sky. Newman slid the agent's pants to his ankles and the boy exhaled a primal sigh. Newman saw himself inching toward the young man's growing erection. He saw the young man's shoulders collapse forward in a shudder of relief as he dropped his gun to the sand.

Newman sprang from the ground, gun in hand. The agent sensed the sudden movement as his fantasy shattered in front of him. He reached for the gun and his pants simultaneously and stumbled forward, his legs ensnared. He caught himself just before the ditch and turned to face Newman.

"Give me that gun, faggot," he snarled.

Newman fired two shots and the agent toppled backwards into the ditch. He was unprepared for the sound the bullets made as they cracked the skull, two sharp and sudden pops, like the snapping of twigs. He walked to the edge of the ditch and peered over. The young man's face was frozen in shock and Newman resisted the urge to ponder his final thoughts. They would engender compassion and compassion, guilt, and so on, and though he despised having to kill a brother in arms he would not feel guilt, not about this. It was him or the kid.

Newman watched himself disrobe and carry his boots and uniform into the ditch. He undressed the agent, then laid the kid's sweat-soaked black suit in pieces on the hood of the town car to dry out before shoveling the displaced sand on top of the body. Newman watched the graceless, cheerless burial and wondered if either version of himself would miss the uniform, or the stars and bars. Perhaps it would sneak up on him like a lost love, and crawl into his consciousness late in the evenings, as he slid from the day into the rye and the books and the darkness, triggered by some innocuous word or image. For the moment, at least, it was little more than an anchor to death from which he was grateful to be unchained.

He patted the top of the grave down with the underside of the shovel and stepped back to see the ocean of sand undisturbed once again. He watched himself say a silent prayer for the young man, but before he could speak to God about himself, before he could offer atonement, he was back inside. He was himself again, and only himself, and the sense of being a spectator to the life of Newman Ginger evaporated as quickly as it had overtaken him an hour before.

He dressed quickly and stepped into the town car. As he spun the car around and sped away he glanced in the rearview mirror and for a brief moment he was certain he saw himself standing over the grave, eyes to God, hands locked in prayer.

Chapter 21

"No chance." Stirrups peered over the small rock ledge of the ridge that wrapped itself around the mountainside, linking all three peaks. Below, in the circular valley sat the Mukhabarat compound wherein twelve of the military's most highly trained covert ops were held captive.

Richards frowned as he looked down on the three hangars that comprised the base. The men were starving, and tempers had grown short, though each did his best to conceal the draining mixture of fear, doubt and hunger that clawed at their insides. They had climbed and jogged some 60 kilometers in less than 48 hours with almost no rest and now, no food.

As each man crested the ridge and crawled to the ridgeline, thought Richards, surely the same realization would overtake them: there was simply no way out.

The brilliance of the base was clear. Three adjacent hangars each lead to a serviceable tarmac on the far side of the compound. Two of the peaks surrounding the base surrendered a thin but passable alley way to the west for flights entering or taking off, but all other approaches and departures would be impossible due to the wind shooting up each face. To attack on foot would force enemy combatants to reveal themselves by approaching down the steep faces, which provided no cover, or through the alley way, which gave the enemy several high points from which to fire down on forces trapped between the two peaks, quite literally shooting fish in a barrel. Should the platoon successfully rescue the SpecOps, they would be left with either of two catastrophic escape options: climb the mountain face and hope they make it back to the ridgeline before the Mukhabarat can counterstrike, or take their chances in the more accessible alley way, where they could be boxed in and held down within a few seconds of entering.

Richards was struck by the absence of aircraft on the tarmac. There was not necessarily a reason for planes to be present, he thought. This would be a difficult center for heavy traffic, obviously. But, three hangars and not one plane? There were only a couple possible explanations- abandonment, possibly. But this was unlikely. The base was too strategically advantageous. Or, perhaps it was a lab of some kind? This would certainly explain why our SpecOps were snooping around, he thought.

"Holy mother of God," said Lincoln as he crawled into position next to Richards. "It's a deathtrap."

The rest of the men made their way to the rock ledge one by one and quietly noted the impossibility of what lay before them. This time Richards did not wait for panic to wash over the platoon.

"Alright, boys, listen up," he began. Again he found himself unsure of the next words, and again chose to simply start with the truth and see where it took him. "It isn't pretty. If those hangars are even moderately staffed, we're outnumbered ten to one. We're out of food. We've lost all communication…" His voice trailed off as he weighed the sum of the facts. "You know how people say, 'worst case scenario,' like it never happens? Well, this is it. It is happening."

"It's a suicide mission," said Brooklyn.

"It's only a suicide mission if we die, Brooklyn," said Richards. "But I don't plan on dying today. I've seen the changes, I know what we're capable of."

Stirrups peered into the valley as a gust of wind howled up the mountainside. "Are we capable of a miracle, boss?"

*

The gate arm flew up at the town car's approach and Newman was instantly back inside the belly of the beast, past the fortified walls and barbwire, past the armed guards and heavy artillery. He drove directly to the tarmac- there would be flights to the north, he would simply have to talk his way onto one.

He stopped on the edge of the tarmac and left the car running. He knew his new uniform- he even adopted the mechanical strut of an agent- allowed him to move through the organized chaos of the working runway system with impunity. The grunts and electricians and mechanics were trained to ignore him, in fact, and the only people who bothered to give him a second glance were the pilots or mid-level leadership, men in positions that often required interaction with black-tie operatives. In the center of it all he saw three grunts boarding a Huey and made a beeline for the chopper

Before he could get ten feet he heard tires squeal and saw a beat-up utility truck barrel through the right angles of the working tarmac directly for him. The truck skid to a halt in front of him. Painted on the side door in fat, joyous strokes was "Smile Time Ice Cream" and beneath it, the slogan, "Eat It."

The side door rolled open and two agents glared down at him. Behind them he could make out the blinking lights and closed circuit monitors of a working security operation and Newman instantly feared the worst: they had tracked the agent as he drove Newman into the desert, they had monitored the grave digging and the sexual advances, and they had surveilled Newman's killing of the young man. They had watched him flip the kid, turn him gay right before their very eyes and surely they would exact some horrific revenge for the double offense of queering up a good man and then killing him. And he had walked right back into their arms. Panic struck and Newman strained to keep the poker face every agent plasters on in training and wears until the day they're buried in an unmarked grave in the Kuwaiti desert.

"Get in," said one of the agents.

Newman hoisted himself into the truck and stifled a grunt, the kind of old man sound he was accustomed to letting slip every time he sat or stood, or exerted himself. One slip, and I'm toast, he thought.

"Bontrager," came a voice from the rear of the truck. The agents took their seats in front of the monitors and suddenly Newman was staring directly at his old friend Bird Dog, a.k.a. General Sydney Fuller, the man who had sent him into the woods so callously, who had betrayed the unspoken code between men who had ascended beyond The Shit, men with stars on their lapels, the scumbag.

"Fuller," said Newman, through grated teeth. If they had been alone he would've shot the old man right there, he thought. He heard the gunshot, saw the shock explode onto Fuller's face as he bolted across the truck bed and wrapped his fingers around the son of a bitch's wrinkled, traitorous throat… But this was a fantasy, he knew. The agents would be upon him instantly, his life would end again, this time for good, and the boys would perish in the mountains.

"Agent Bontrager," began Fuller, "Iraq is once again threatening an attack on our good friends in Israel. In Saddam's paranoid, delusional fantasy they've labeled it a preemptive strike in some ever-impending war." Fuller guffawed. "Preemptive strike! Do you believe that? These dictators, they think they can get away with murder!"

As Fuller expounded on the illegalities of a so-called preemptive strike and the audacity of tyrants, Newman sat stone-faced, perplexed that Sydney had no recognition of him. Was the new uniform so powerful that a friend of thirty years could somehow be masked? Hidden behind a black tie and sunglasses? Or was the military so contextual, so cleft, so segregated that once a man changed his shirt he became someone else entirely? All Sydney had to do was take one look at the man to whom he was speaking and he would know. Yet, he blathers on, thought Newman. He does not see me.

"These Iraqi threats have always been toothless," said Fuller. "Until now. We found something. A regime element, recently granted political asylum, has alerted us to the possible existence of actionable nuclear arms."

Newman snapped to attention. For the moment, at least, he decided it would be best to pay attention, and he would return to plotting Fuller's demise later.

"There is a cache of three weaponized warheads somewhere in Iraq," said Fuller. "This time, Bontrager, the threat is real."

Newman swallowed hard. He was exhilarated to know he was so close to the action. Since 1983 he kept a duffel in the trunk of his car on the off-chance he got the call. Just a few short weeks ago he begged this same man for an assignment in The Shit, something real, away from the desks and the paperwork and the shackles of old age, and it was here. It was now. It was happening. But Fuller had sent him into the woods. And Fuller's superiors had sent him into the mountains, and then into the desert. They had discarded him, along with six other men. Those men tried to help him. The throw-aways had carried him up a mountainside to safety on their backs. They rescued him from a bloodthirsty mob. They gave a shit. He must get back to them.

"Once you're inside," began Fuller…

"Inside?" said Newman.

"There is no turning back. Do not leave until you've relayed the coordinates."

"Relayed…" he began, but was jolted by the truck's sudden stop. Before he could continue the side door was whipped open and two men dressed as cocktail waiters reached into the truck bed, grabbed him and ripped him out. They were Iraqi, possibly former military, strong and lean. They had him by the arms and one man placed his hand over Newman's mouth, the other wrapped his arm around Newman's waist and together they carried him through unmarked double doors and into a wide hallway.

They whisked him past open doors and Newman caught glimpses of the cavernous rooms and halls that branched from this service hallway. They passed an industrial kitchen as it bustled with chefs and waiters, squash courts with dimmed lights, and a garage the size of an airplane hangar stuffed with late model cars. They stopped at the end of the hallway and set Newman down while they fiddled with the door lock.

Newman looked to his right and saw the edge of a table, but something about the table seemed off: It was wooden, not an operating table; It was surrounded by a few small pools of liquid, not chairs, clearly not a serving table.

He elbowed past the cocktail waiters and stepped into the room. He saw the chains first. Draped over the ends of the table, the silver inch-thick chains were caked with dried, purple-brown blood. They just hung there lifelessly, innocent of the crimes at which they hinted. He caught glimpses of other devices in the shadows but came back to the chains. He used chains to tie down furniture in a flatbed pickup, or to lock the gates around Edwards. They were supposed to hold the world together.

Newman jumped when one of the waiters grabbed him by the arm and spun him around. He was led into a small back office where a waiter began to strip him of his clothes, while the other attempted to dress him in a waiter's uniform. They hastily taped a microphone to his chest and tucked a receiver into his underwear before Newman screamed for them to stop molesting him, he could dress himself. As he buttoned the new uniform, it occurred to him that he could not sink much lower. He had gone from a decorated general in the United States armed forces to a servant-class Iraqi cocktail monkey in only a few weeks. Sure, he thought, he was under cover, but only a handful of people in the world knew that, and they were all sitting in an ice cream truck half a mile away. If the shit hit the fan, he thought, they would be halfway to Kuwait by the time he escaped.

The waiters handed him a tray of hors d'oeuvres and shoved him through double doors, and the noise of it all came crashing onto him. Dignitaries and wives in ball gowns, silverware on plates, hard shoes against the floor and chatter, the endless chatter spotted with bursts of laughter and joyous exclamations. Could they hear any of this back in the van, over the thumping bass kick of his heartbeat, he wondered?

He made his way to the enormous plate glass windows that overlooked the garage. As he squeezed through the crowd men and women frowned at him as they snatched the tiny canapes from his tray. He didn't give the scowling panjandrum a second glance, at first to keep cover and then because he was too distracted by the seven columns of late model, foreign limousines below. Valets whipped more long, black limos into place at the end of each column, one after another as guests poured in, and Newman watched as they raised the enormous metal door at the far end and locked it in place. The hangar was so full, they would not be able to lower the door until the guests departed, hours from now.

"You like what you see," came a man's voice from behind Newman. "That one's mine," he said, and a long, thin finger pointed a golden sports car in the center of the hangar. "Porsche." Newman felt the taller man's hot breath on his neck. "Finest European sports car available today," whispered the man. "A gift from my father."

Newman felt the phlegm catch in his throat. He prayed that his eyes did not reveal the terror in his heart.

"You don't look familiar to me," continued the man in stilted English. "You have very fair skin." Newman felt the man press his body against him. "I like fair skin."

Newman began to turn his head toward the hot breath of the man now pressed against him but was stopped short.

"Don't look at me," barked the man, and Newman froze. "Meet me at the gold Porsche in thirty minutes and I'll take you for a spin. Tell the guards Uday sent you."

Newman felt the man's body drift away and suddenly the buzz of the room flooded back into his consciousness. He felt himself exhale and wiped the sweat from his temples with the stiff sleeve of his uniform.

"My god," he muttered to himself. "We are all gay."

"What is that," said Fuller, helpless in the truck. "Is that code? He looked to the agents, who shrugged.

*

Newman scanned the hangar for signs of the valets, but they had scattered like rats the moment Newman entered. They had developed a sixth sense for Uday's beastly presence, he must've claimed waitstaff at events like this before, and they knew how to look busy in just such a way that fleeing appeared to be in service of the son of Saddam, as opposed to in terror of him.

Newman was at once mortified and a touch flattered that Uday had picked him out of the crowd. He reasoned that he must have been giving off some signal, perhaps some pheromone that alerted the other gays to his presence. If this was true, then perhaps he did absorb the gas, perhaps the scientist was right. The possibility raised so many questions- Is it getting worse? Is it permanent? Can it be masked by clothing, or cologne, perhaps a topical ointment?- that he did not notice Uday approaching until the despot placed his hand on Newman's lower back.

He had come to collect his prize. When Newman spun to face him Uday lunged forward for a kiss. Newman reflexively palmed the prince's face and thrust him backwards into a nearby Renault. Instantly Newman's cover was blown. The impact set off the car's alarm and sent Uday into a wild-eyed rage. He lunged at Newman again and again the general deflected the attack, grabbing the prince's wrist and using his momentum to whip him around and into the gold Porsche head-first, setting of that car's alarm and knocking Uday unconscious. Guests from the soirée above gathered at the huge windows overlooking the garage, aghast at this waiter's treasonous attack on the prince. Newman knew he had only seconds before Uday's security forces caught wind and descended upon the garage, he had only a few seconds to commit to the escape.

He leapt into the gold Porsche and found the keys still in the ignition. He closed his eyes, inhaled deeply and turned the key. The car roared to life. He reached down to shift gears and slid his left foot to the clutch but hit only the baseboards. He lifted his foot and pressed down again, and again hit only the baseboards. He looked to his right hand and was shocked to see it resting on an automatic transmission. There was no stick. There was no clutch. Newman chuckled to himself- this precision automobile had been customized-neutered- for the little prince who could not drive a stick.

Newman shifted into drive and gently lowered his toes onto the gas pedal. The gold Porsche shot forward and slammed directly into a parked limousine. Newman gasped for breath. He was whiplashed before he had even left the hangar.

In front of him, valets began to warily filter back into the facility, hastened by the loud crash. Behind him, state security forces in plainclothes burst into the garage and began searching frantically for the prince. Newman reversed, then dropped the car back into drive. He pressed the pedal to the baseboard and held on for his life. The car tore into the midday sun as bullets ricocheted off its armor plating.

Within minutes Newman found himself on a jam-packed four-lane road in the busiest section of Baghdad. Suddenly cars began pulling off the road for him to pass. Delivery vans chugged onto side streets and squat, decrepit hatchbacks veered into abandoned parking lots to create room across all four lanes. The sea of sand-covered cars parted, the world for all but him came to a standstill, and Newman gunned the engine as he passed to maintain his cover as Iraq's tyrannical prince. No one looked, but everyone saw the gold Porsche, and within minutes Newman was out of the city and headed north at 150 kilometers per hour.

*

The Elder hung his prayer rug over the camel tie. The hitching post for the town's beasts of burden was empty, a stark reminder of the offenses visited upon him only a few days earlier. He had done his best to return to normalcy- awoke before sunrise, prayed five times each day, visited his great-grandchildren- though all he wanted to do was curl into a ball and die. He had lived a long life- so long, in fact, he had lost count of the years- and the incident had left him to ponder the meaning of all his collected years and wisdom, if there was a meaning. After all, what good was a life well spent if it was to lead to humiliation in its closing act.

There was, however, little room in his heart for revenge- he did not have the energy for it. Instead, he decided, he would forgive the old American who had acted so monstrously in the hopes that through forgiveness he could find the peace to continue, at least until Abra, his favorite great-grandchild was bequeathed to a husband.

Allah, give me the strength to forgive, or at least to forget, he whispered to himself. The vanity of fury was unbecoming for a man of his age and wisdom, he knew, and he called on the highest power and was received, and suddenly blessed. He felt Allah's hands holding his, stroking his wiry hair, and peace became him.

He noticed two young boys set their AK-47's down to chase one of the town's stray dogs, but the mutt was slick. It raced to the well in the center of town for a buttress, then led the boys in circles around the well, its tongue wagging. The boys chased it side by side, blindly, always just close enough to see its hind legs. Finally the boys split up and one went left and one went right and a hair's breath before they descended on the dog, the dirty mutt leapt onto the lip of the well and pranced around to the other side. The boys collided into one another, the head of one boy slamming into the knee of the other, tears streamed, and suddenly they were chasing each other and hurtling death threats while the dirt-covered mutt watched on.

The elder felt a tinge of pride. These boys would make excellent soldiers someday, he thought. They stumbled, but they did not fall. Instead they found their footing and resumed the fight. Albeit, against one another, but still, he thought, they resumed the fight.

It was this fortitude that kept him and his children alive, he recalled, as they fled southern Iraq, when the monster, Saddam Hussein took power. He and his brothers stumbled, but did not fall. The will to fight, to die for their beliefs was the reason he was still alive, and the reason Kurdish Sunni'ism was still alive, and the reason these boys could live to fight for themselves. He still wore the gun- the strap over his bony left shoulder, the chamber bouncing lazily off his lower back as he ambled around town- as a reminder of the sacrifices one must make to protect one's family against the tyranny of powerful men.

The mere passing thought of that living horror, Saddam, shook the elder, and he gripped the camel tie to ground himself. He would give his last breaths to see the demise of the tyrant, the blaspheme whose excesses were legendary, and outshone only by his cruelty. Rumor had it that his sons were waking nightmares of torture and murder, too. Though the elder had not fired a gun in some ten years- the kickback was too jarring against his wilted frame- he swam in the adrenaline that coursed trough his spidery veins at the thought of carving out the eyes of those Shiite dogs with bullets from his battle-tested AK-47.

Tires shredded the dirt at the edge of town, and the elder looked for the source of the commotion. It was rare that any vehicle reached Zhakoudahouk, rarer still that it was not a local militia transport of some kind, looking to pass peacefully. Few travelers dared approach the bombed-out huts and hostile clans that occupied the satellite villages spread through the region. Only the bravest, or most arrogant… He spotted the golden sports car as it turned onto the main stretch leading to the village center, the well. He could not believe his eyes.

"Uday," he muttered to himself. "Uday!" His heart thumped against his chest and through his throat, into his ears and behind his eyes. He called again, this time at the top of his lungs, "Uday! Uday!"

For the young boys, it was a siren call to arms. They were raised on bedtime stories wherein the traditional ghosts and bogeymen were swapped out for Hussein family members. Every illness, death, and misfortune in the village and even the country was attributable to the monstrous clan Hussein, and they had come to regard the mythical three-headed monster- Saddam, Uday and Qusay- as kin to Iblis, the devil himself. Suddenly they were thrust into their own dreams, a transcendent moment without precedent: a chance to slay the dragon.

They came running from the shadows and scrambled to separate their guns, which had become tangled in the rush to catch the stray dog. They tugged at the weapons and pushed each other away, unable to loose the clips and butts from the criss-crossed straps. The elder remembered his own weapon and reached for it. The calls of "Uday!" continued largely to himself as he fiddled with the clip and the safety with trembling fingers. A red curtain fell over his eyes, and as the gold Porsche skidded to a stop in front of the well the elder whooped and lashed his tongue up and down against the roof of his mouth, the historic battle cry of his ancestors, and pulled the trigger.

*

Newman heard the distinct, terrifying pop and simultaneous crack of the automatic rifle before he saw the shooter. He had overheard colleagues and other war dogs talk about the two sounds that define the AK blast, and to a man they could recall the exact moment, months and even years into battle when they were first able to hear both. Those who spent enough time in The Shit could hear, distinctly, the bass hit of the round leaving the chamber and the simultaneous crack of the instant echo made by gas exploding to eject the spent round. The civilian brain could process only one, he knew- the pop or the crack- and only seasoned war dogs could remain calm enough, focused enough, to hear both, so it came as a shock to him that suddenly, decades after leaving The Shit, he was finally able to hear both pieces of the deadly call. Now, after all these years, with senses dulled by age and drink and life…

One gun had turned to three, he could hear, and a thunderous shower of pops and cracks were accompanied by the dull thuds of bullets hitting the armored car. The vehicle rocked and creaked as it was dotted by round after round. Sooner or later the armor plating would give way, he knew- vehicles were outfitted to survive a barrage in order to give the driver enough time to escape, not an onslaught while the driver cowered and prayed. He knew he must move, now.

Newman ducked to his right and crawled across the front seat, and out the passenger door. He quickly rolled to the front tire, hoping it would shield him from the ricochets that were known to take out shins and knees. He had discovered a small pistol in the glove box somewhere north of Baghdad to replace the one the waiters had stolen as they dressed him for the party, but knew he would be shredded to pieces the moment he stood to fire. He was trapped. Should even one villager emerge from any of the huts or alleys on this side of the car, he was finished, pinned down on both sides.

Suddenly the shooting stopped and the car rocked to a halt, its fractured joints and crushed steel letting out a death wail. Smoke and dirt swirled around him and he knew he had only a few short seconds to make a move while the villagers reloaded. He could run, he knew, but the huts and alleys- should he reach them- offered little protection against three furious gunmen. He would have to face his attackers, to call a truce on the good name and faith of the United States of America.

"American!" he cried. "American!"

The two boys looked to the elder and repeated the call, and the elder lowered his weapon. "American?"

"American," called Newman, as he raised his empty hands above the hood of the car, and slowly stood, arms above his head, two peace signs now formed with trembling fingers. With his sunglasses and wrinkled black suit, and black tie, he looked like a mod Nixon as he shouted again, "American!"

The assailants lowered their weapons to get a better look at the American, and it struck Newman that two of the gunmen were just boys, no more than 10. What the hell were they so mad about, thought Newman?

As the dust settled, the elder's eyes widened "Camel thief! Camel thief!" he screamed, and resumed firing on Newman.

Newman didn't have time to play it cool, to pretend there was some misunderstanding. He dove to the ground as bullets cascaded against the crumbling frame. He peered under the car and saw the boys drop to the ground as well. They were shrewd, the little bastards. They were going to drop him from below.

He pulled himself up and dove back into the car, climbing into the back seat, looking for more cover than the crippled front panels could provide. He wedged himself down into the foot space to get away from the windows but couldn't find the floor. Strange lumps of plastic and paper covered the floorboards and through the tinted darkness Newman could make out magazines, everywhere, magazines. He swam through them to the floorboards when his hands came upon several soft plastic packages. He rolled onto his back and held the package to the fractured light from the rear window, where he saw, to his amazement, the image of a western-looking man standing behind a bent over blowup sex doll.

He dropped the package and reached for another- also a blowup sex doll- and a third, and a fourth. He grabbed one of the magazines: *Hustler*. He held it to the light from the window and the thought crossed his mind that for the first time in his life, he felt no guilt, no shame or anger when holding a smut magazine, only the slightest sense of erotic rush- not from the women, but from the suggestion of pleasure, of urges met, that holding the magazine suggested.

The tiny side windows exploded inward and he shielded his eyes from the thick black glass. It would be a matter of seconds before those little shits were at the window firing in, he thought. He pulled himself into the front seat and rolled out onto the ground again. He could hear the boys and the elder shout to one another as they reloaded. He knew in a few short seconds, the boys would make their move and he would have no cover this time.

"Wait!" he screamed. "Wait!" He leapt up, arms outstretched, his empty palms facing the boys, who, for all their bloodlust, were still boys: they were game. They would put any beating on pause to hear the cries and negotiations of their victim. If the offer was weak, or antagonistic, the beating would resume immediately. For Newman, a poor offering would be fatal. He reached into the backseat and pulled out the only olive branch he had: high-end, red-blooded American porn.

Newman waved two of the magazines above his head, one in each hand and began to shuffle around the front of the wheezing, whistling car. "Free," he called. "Free!"

The boys froze. Even from a distance they could delineate the unbroken curves of a naked, full figured woman. They lowered their weapons and shuffled across the town square like starved dogs, wary of the strange man and his offering. Newman lowered the magazines to eye level, bringing the boys face to face with the huge pink nipples, disappearing torso and smooth, cream-colored legs of their first cover girl. They snatched the magazines from his hands and dropped their guns to the ground. They spoke excitedly in Arabic and gestured wildly with their hands in front of their chests, and made universal symbols of appreciation for the model's gifts.

The elder approached, approving of the offering, and Newman dropped to his knees in front of him.

"Help."

Ryan Gielen

Chapter 22

Richards lay flat on his belly fifty meters from the ridgeline. Twenty meters to his right lay Chico and then Stirrups, fifty meters to his left, Deadweight, Lincoln and Brooklyn. They had stashed whatever gear remained and began their approach with only moderate cover culled from the tall grass and dirt that lined the mountainside. Richards had calculated correctly that with only an hour until sunset, the men must get off the ridgeline and get in position before the base's day patrols returned and night patrols left for the evening. The men felt no small rush as camel-backed and foot soldiers wove through them unknowingly on their way to the opposite faces of the mountain. At nightfall, they would make their approach and in the darkest hour, the dead of night when most were asleep, they would breach the compound. It was timed perfectly, Richards knew, only insomuch as it gave his boys their only chance of survival. Six men against a compound's worth was, as each of the men had pointed out, a death sentence, and to breach the compound any earlier would mean fighting a hundred elite soldiers on their own turf.

Richards heard a grunting, heaving noise on the ridgeline above him and carefully spun a few degrees back toward the source. His stomach sank as he saw the first camel's head peer over the ridge. Iad and the villagers had finally caught up. This ragtag collection of gun wielding farmers and long-former soldiers would surely draw the attention of the men in the compound. For a fleeting second Richards considered turning his men on Iad's and wiping out the threat before their presence reached the Mukhabarat, but he couldn't afford to initiate a fire fight from below against the wrong enemy, an enemy whose anger he could empathize with, being that it was directed almost entirely at General Newman Ginger.

The villagers flooded the ridgeline now, thirty in all, camelback, with AK-47's draped across their laps and ammunition flung over their shoulders. Their focus was a hundred meters below, past the hidden platoon, at the entrance to the hangars. They expected to catch the Americans attempting to enter the compound, at which point a few well-placed mortar rounds would wake the sleeping Mukhabarat, trapping the platoon between an onslaught of elite Iraqi fighters and the villagers who would hold the high ground of the ridgeline.

Richards signaled to his men to hold their position. They would stick with the plan until or unless they were spotted from above, where Iad's men- 30, to Richards' six- would have the distinct advantage of the ridgeline perch.

Below, a Mukhabarat soldier emerged from the near hangar, lit a cigarette, and looked to the sky. Richards watched the man bask for a moment in the crisp evening air, and stretch his arms high above his head. As he stretched he closed his eyes and Richards envied his cluelessness. The man, in that moment, was at peace. He was in the middle of a shift, not a mission. He was not fixated on killing or surviving, his body and mind completely free of the stress of knowing he could be ending or defending life at any second. When this is all over, thought Richards, I'm going to open a flower shop where no one knows my name.

The Mukhabarat soldier slowly lowered his arms and exhaled. He opened his eyes. Instead of lifting his cigarette to his mouth, however, he stood completely still, arms at his side. He squinted. He began to scream.

*

Newman saw the first sparks of light on the distant ridgeline and feared the worst. Each crisp yellow-orange explosion from the muzzles of the AK-47's expanded and contracted against the night sky in an instant, a thousand collapsing stars, each with the potential to suck his boys into the black hole left in their wake. He begged god for more, knowing his boys lasted as long as the gunshots did.

Crammed into the Porsche with him were the village elder and the young boys. The boys passed the smut magazines back and forth as the elder gripped the door handle and center console in a failed attempt to remain calm. He was at home in battle, but it had been 40 years since he rode in a motorized vehicle, and then only once. He was simply not prepared for the leap from camel to precision automobile.

Newman wove through the parked camels and skidded to a stop at the entrance to the ridgeline. The villagers spun, startled by the headlights, and three men ran toward the vehicle while the rest of the ragtag militia continued to fire down the mountainside on what Newman assumed were his platoon.

The village boys began to tug at their door handles and Newman had to bark at them to hold still. They may be his only cards, he knew. He shoved the elder out of the car, and the two sentries immediately lowered their weapons. Newman stepped out, hands empty and high. The sentries raised their guns again, bewildered by the sight of the crazed camel thief, who was supposed to be below them in the compound.

Just around the bend, at the edge of the ridgeline, Newman could make out the mercenary, the key to his salvation and the safety of his boys, Iad.

"Iad!" he called through the crossfire. "Iad!"

Iad drew his weapon at the sight of Newman, and charged through the villagers, but a sickening thud stopped him in his tracks. Newman heard the splitting of skin and the crack of bone and ligament, each horrifying crack, one by one. Iad's arm dropped to his side and he fell to one knee. Newman ran to him, and helped him to the ground as the villagers and the elder surrounded him and poured water from their canteens over his head and face.

"Iad," cried Newman. "Are you…"

Iad lifted his right arm to reveal a rapidly widening bloodstain. "My men are outnumbered, ten to one," he groaned. "You have led us to annihilation."

"I've come to make peace," said Newman. "I've come to help."

Iad coughed as the blood crawled up to his shoulder and down to his waist. "Only Allah can help us now."

The elder pulled feebly at Newman's shoulders, and the sentries clamored to remove the blood-soaked shirt. One of the sentries accidentally caught Newman with a sharp elbow to the mouth and he tumbled backwards. Newman watched for a moment as they discarded the dying man's clothes. He noticed the CIA-issued night-vision binoculars had been thrown from Iad's belt as it was pulled from his body.

Newman made the sign of the cross for the dying man, and thought, God forgive him, as I have. He grabbed the binoculars and bolted for the ridgeline, and fell to his stomach as bullets flew around him. He stared down, seeing black and green impressions of the Mukhabarat at the base of the mountain, much of it blotted out by the gunfire that read white-hot through the binoculars. The Mukhabarat were quickly adapting. The bullet sprays had no hope of arcing down onto the crouching villagers, tucked safely behind the ridgeline, and two shoulder-mounted rocket launchers were rounded up. They would blow the ridge to hell and expose the villagers, or cause enough damage above the ridge to maim the unprotected tribesmen. Newman felt the noose tighten.

As the first rocket was launched, however, Newman jerked his gaze up the mountainside to avoid the punch of light and was shocked to see several figures laying in the tall grass and reeds. The streaking rocket provided a few seconds of clarity but not enough to tell whether the bodies were corpses or just frozen in waiting. Newman fixed his gaze on the mountain side and when the next rocket launched, he caught several of the figures pointedly stop their movement down the mountain just as the rocket passed, so as not to give away their approach under the passing glare of the rocket's trail.

Newman knew there would be no way to reach them, no way to beg them to hold, or turn back. The only way was forward. Always forward. He heard the death wails of Iad behind him and ran back to say goodbye.

"We are outnumbered," lamented Iad. "I have led these men like lambs to slaughter. And for what," he asked. "For what prize?"

"What was that," asked Newman.

"I have wasted these men! For vanity, for power, for hatred!"

"No, before that!"

"We are outnumbered," cried Iad, growing irritated. "We are outnumbered ten to one! We are all going to die!"

Newman leapt to his feet, barely able to contain his excitement. "We're outnumbered! We're outnumbered!" He dropped the binoculars at Iad's side, gave the dying man's outstretched hand a final squeeze, and ran to the car.

*

Richards distrusted the silence. He peered to his right and caught Chico and Stirrups staring back, awaiting the next go signal. To his left he knew Brooklyn,

Lincoln and Deadweight awaited his command as well, but something in his gut told him to hold. He lifted his head and peered down what remained of the mountain-side. They were only forty meters from the compound and he could make out the huddling Mukhabarat, re-grouping. This could mean only one thing: the villagers had retreated. The better-trained, better-equipped mer-cenaries would shortly advance, up the hill and over the ridgeline, until they had tracked down and killed every one of the villagers, and to reach the villagers, they would plow through the platoon.

He ran through his options. Retreat, never. They would be slaughtered the moment they moved more quickly than the grass in which they currently cowered. Advance, impossible. The base had emptied and fifty elite, armed men stood ready to defend it, already keyed up from their practice run with the local farmers and goat herders. Hold, catastrophic. The Mukhabarat would either advance on the hill and stumble upon the six platoon members now, or those who remained on night-watch would discover them at first light, when their camouflage would not have the aid of night.

A Mukhabarat scream broke his concentration. He gripped his weapon and looked through the site, certain they had been spotted, but the frantic soldier pointed to the northern ridgeline, some 300 meters away. Suddenly the entire Mukhabarat force raced to the northeast wall of the building, readying arms and calling commands to one another. Richards was dumbfounded. The platoon looked to him for the go signal but he carefully shifted his body and weapon to face the northern ridgeline, figuring he would like to be certain that this was not some simple trap designed to draw his men into revealing their position.

Richards did not- would not- believe his eyes. Atop the ridgeline, which sat on the rim of a mountain range in the northern hills of Iraq- a rare, dead corner of earth so antiquated and forgotten by time and man that even its own countrymen viewed it as a land of ghosts- stood what appeared to be a western-style blowup doll, with her hands on her hips as if to intentionally push out her small, triangular breasts, and full, lipsticked mouth opened to a perfect circle, which seemed to suggest she was just as surprised as he was to find her there.

He pulled his eyes from the site and blinked- he was starved and exhausted, and now, it seemed, hallucinatory. He peered through the site again and saw a second! And a third! The Mukhabarat fanned out and opened fire on the rapidly multiplying enemy, but each time a doll would drop another would spring up meters away. The Mukhabarat were incensed. The enemy appeared to be vast and growing.

He was too stunned to examine the absurdity of it all, and quickly threw a "go" signal to his right and left. The men stood and charged down the hill. Richards reached the hangar door first and tore it from its hinges, and the men poured into the compound, weapons drawn.

He threw the door aside and peered through his site to the northeastern ridgeline again. Doll after doll popped up with the same cruel, mock expression of shock, then was quickly mowed down by bullets from below. It was a carnival game from hell for the Mukhabarat, who were infuriated by their inability to intimidate these goat herders by felling their comrades the instant one showed his head. He gave one final look to the southeastern mountainside and observed a band of villagers- in a final stroke of genius- silently blitzing down the empty face, weapons drawn. The entire scene unfolded in his mind's eye: the distracted Mukhabarat would be assaulted from the rear, splintered, then sniped from above as the blowup dolls were exhausted and the villagers moved to the front line. Some would surrender; some would vanish into the hills, only returning to pillage whatever stores remained in the hangars. Most would be killed.

He caught up to the platoon just inside the first building. Together they continued past the mess hall and offices. Before moving onto the second building, Richards peered into the hangar itself, expecting to see fuel hoses, utility jeeps and military aircraft, but to his surprise it was empty, abandoned. It struck him that the offices and mess were strangely empty and unused as well. He could not recall a single computer or phone, papers, signs of life. A small knot began to form in his stomach. The second hangar brought no relief- it appeared to be little more than a parking garage for a small cadre of vehicles. By now Richards was certain the compound was used for little more than a way station, an outpost for various missions, and if so, it was highly unlikely that his SpecOps brothers would be imprisoned here. No security force in their right mind would attempt to drag American elite fighters from black site to black site, exposing them to the outside world, to the inevitable rescue parties, introducing variables like weather and civilians which would provide opportunities to be exploited by the SpecOps themselves. No, they would find a bunker near one of the military arteries of the country, bury the men under and behind as much steel and concrete as possible, and wait. They would live in and around the space, making the security of the bunker and the captivity of the men their prerogative. This compound, on the other hand, appeared to be built and maintained solely for launching attacks from the northern tip of the country, meant to service large but transient forces and their arsenal. So, he wondered, what was in the Mukhabarat's arsenal?

*

Newman handed the final blowup doll to the village elder who appeared to experience a mix of shame and bafflement at the plan, despite its success. There was something undignified, unmanly about this tactic, though he had given it his blessing when the camel thief explained, correctly, that they would be slaughtered should they attempt to fight the Mukhabarat by traditional means.

Newman signaled the band of villagers to attack from the southeastern ridgeline and watched as they slid into striking distance behind the assembled, oblivious Mukhabarat. Once they were in position he flashed the headlights of the Porsche three times and the men of the ridgeline picked up their weapons and began to fire. As the Mukhabarat began to return the volley, the stealth force behind them opened fire as well. It was a bloodbath. Mukhabarat scrambled like cockroaches in every direction. Handfuls escaped into the valleys around the hangar- they would have to be dispatched with by local tribesmen at some point, but for now the villagers were free to lick their wounds and retreat safely into the mountains.

Newman witnessed the massacre with a mix of pride and horror, suddenly grateful to have spent the last thirty years of his career in a drab office building in San Bernardino. He was outside himself again, and he watched himself reflect without glory on the destruction in front of him. He watched himself, victorious without joy, just a man at work and his job well done. For the briefest moment he glimpsed a future at peace with himself, having proven he could still lead, still inspire, still matter.

A distant rumbling broke his reflection and he was one again. The sound of rolling thunder reverberated off the walls of the valley and created the dizzying effect that the mountains themselves were awaking, roused by the pesky gunfire. It grew louder with each passing second and a knot quickly formed in Newman's stomach. There was only one thing that hummed through the sky with such consistency and it came with a payload big enough to scorch the mountains, the valley and every camel within a thousand meters. He suddenly became very aware of the distance between him and his boys, staggering around blindly, deep within the empty compound.

*

Richards led his men through the third and final wing of the compound, and found it almost as barren as the previous two. The men stopped at the mess, where the first signs of life appeared: tables covered in emptied, strewn MRE's, duffel bags along the wall and a few large radios. This was the temporary home of the mobile force currently being thrashed outside, and it only confirmed what he already suspected: this was a unit on the move, a transport team, not a hunkered-down prison unit. He signaled the men forward and as they reached the final door in the long hallway leading to the final hangar, he overtook them, determined to clear the hangar himself, quickly, and get his boys out and into the mountains before they had time to realize just how bamboozled they had been. He kicked the door in in one swift motion and he and the men burst into the hangar.

They were greeted by three enormous flatbed trucks parked end-to-end and a half-dozen armored humvees, confirming once and for all that they had stumbled upon a simple convoy.

The men stopped, baffled. "This is no prison," called Brooklyn.

"What the hell are we doing here?" screamed Stirrups.

Lincoln and Chico agreed and the men staggered around and cursed the mission while Richards tried to calm their frayed nerves. At the far end of the hangar the door collapsed as Newman kicked his way in, and the men ran toward him, guns drawn.

"Stop!" he called. "It's me!"

"You!" Richards howled. "You son of a bitch! You knew! You knew all along!"

"I came back as soon as I knew," yelled Newman.

"Wait one second," yelled Stirrups. "Knew what?" He glared from Newman to Richards, furious.

Richards finally broke the silence. "There were no SpecOps," he said. "It was a set up, a…" his voice trailed off.

"A suicide mission," said Newman. "We were sent here to disappear."

"*We* were sent here to disappear," cried Stirrups, "*you* were saved!"

"But, I'm back!" he pleaded.

"Why?" asked Richards.

"Who cares," yelled Stirrups. "He left us, now we leave him. Let's go!" He turned and marched toward the exterior door through which Newman had come, as the first streams of pale blue daylight spilled through.

"I'm here to rescue you," Newman called after him. "I'm here to rescue you!"

"From what," Richards shouted, over the curses and protestations of his men. "From what?"

At that exact moment, the not-so-distant rumbling that had startled Newman on the ridgeline grew to a swell, as the screech of F-16 jet engines tore overhead.

"Who called for backup," asked Lincoln.

"SatComm link is dead," said Richards.

"That ain't backup," cried Newman. "Get on the trucks! Now!"

The men bolted for the first truck. Brooklyn and Chico ripped the enormous tarp from the bed of the truck and stumbled backwards, shocked by what they saw. The SS-19 Intercontinental Ballistic Missile was capable of threading a needle at 5,000 miles, contained six warheads, and currently sat perched on the back of what Newman had hoped would be an escape vehicle for his boys when the F-16's turned around for their first strafing run. Newman pushed through the men to get a closer look and saw a hint of yellow paint through the dirt caked onto the side of the rocket. He spit on his hand and ran it along the missile shaft. As the dirt fell away the men gasped at the yellow and black nuclear symbol adorning the missile, a hastily painted mother of all warnings.

The F-16's screamed overhead again followed by two earth-shaking explosions at the far end of the compound. The walls were closing in on the platoon, and they knew it. Someone began reciting the Lord's Prayer. Lincoln took kneeled on the ground to steady himself.

"Okay, next truck," said Newman. He and Richards moved to the second truck and ripped the tarp off. Newman spit on his hand and wiped it along the missile, and again revealed the yellow and black nuclear symbol. Stirrups screamed.

"Okay, next truck," Newman said again.

In less than two minutes they would become collateral damage, he knew. Even with their heightened strength and speed, on foot they would not make it to the ridgeline in time to take cover. Should they escape in the vehicles, they would give the F-16's juicy, cumbersome targets, they would be sitting ducks. They were trapped.

He refused to believe it was over. They were supposed to be the most talented fighting force the world had ever known, an invincible, supernatural gift from the gods. It was irreconcilable with the reality that they were going to die in this hangar like helpless strays.

The world slowed, as if his mind were clinging to sanity by photographing every frame individually, and playing it back for him in quarter-time to prove that he was still here, a last-ditch effort to deny the inevitable. Every sense was attenuated- the scents of diesel fuel and sawdust filled his nostrils; The cold steel of the third missile stung his calloused fingers; The sound of the jet engines, once disappeared, now whistled from just a few miles away, and cut through the confused calls of his men.

His men. Where were they? He turned. Stirrups ambled toward him from across the hangar. Richards was here, awaiting instructions. Lincoln and Brooklyn closed ranks and Chico, too. Deadweight, thought Newman. Where the hell was that slovenly lump of…

"Hey guys," called Deadweight.

The men turned toward the voice of the rotund private, but he was nowhere to be seen. "Up here," he whispered.

They looked up and to their astonishment, Deadweight floated above them, arms outstretched, suspended in flight.

Chico fainted into Stirrups' arms. Lincoln and Brooklyn stared, shocked. Richards looked to Newman, hoping the old man might have some secret wisdom, some experience that would illuminate exactly what to do when a platoon mate took flight. Newman was aghast.

Ryan Gielen

Chapter 23

Major Captain Arthur "Artie" Harris had provided air support and security over hot zones in the Middle East for almost a decade. He had passed on three opportunities to retire to the private sector, where he could have immediately cashed in on his extensive training and experience to receive a six-figure salary flying for any of the world's airlines. Instead he chose to re-up with the Air Force each time, believing the containment of the Hussein regime to be far more important than his own comfort. In truth, however, he was only comfortable when flying in war zones, so the decision to re-up was never in question. He moved his wife and three children to an American outpost in Germany in order to be closer to them during his leave, and though they missed him, they forgave him for his passion and were always grateful for the time they had together. Artie firmly believed he had been in the service so long, and flown so many runs, he had seen everything.

"Five klicks and closing, Fox Trot," said Artie. Their first run cleared the airspace, and their second run had taken out two-thirds of the compound. This would be their third and final run, the deathblow.

"Copy, Yankee Delta, five klicks," responded his wingman, Hillman. "Let's bomb this tent back to the stone age." Tent was the derogatory term they had taken to using for the undermanned military installations they discovered in the mountains of the north and the border deserts of the east and west, because they crumpled like paper under bombing, and the Mukhabarat never bothered- or couldn't afford- to build safe, durable bunkers underneath. What you saw was what you got, and what you got was easy to fold onto itself.

"Lock," said Artie.

"Lock."

"Fire."

"Fire."

The clusters of AGM-65 Mavericks ripped through the sky and obliterated the hangars below. Artie caught the reflection of the fireball below in his rearview mirror, the cockpit glass.

"Target liberated," he called.

No response came.

"Copy, Fox Trot?" he asked, as an urgency crept into his voice.

Again, no response came. Artie glanced down to his Horizontal Situation Indicator to confirm Hillman's position. The second F-16 was still on his wing and trailing by a quarter klick, but a new bird had appeared. Artie's heart skipped a beat- they had cleared the airspace, and besides, the Mukhabarat had no planes on the tarmac, or in the northern half of the country as far as the U.S. Air Force could tell. This was supposed to be an uncontested victory, a simple early morning sweep.

"Fox Trot, you…" his voice trailed off. Three more birds appeared on the HSI. "Fox Trot, what the hell is going on back there?" he barked.

"Yankee Delta," came Hillman's voice, soft and shaken. "You better have a look at this."

Artie eased the throttle and the plane slowed until Hillman was directly on his wing. He followed Hillman's gaze across both planes to the east and at first saw nothing. He looked back to Hillman, afraid the depressurization mechanism in his bird had failed. Hillman's eyes suddenly grew wider, and Artie looked again to the east and saw what his wingman had been so mesmerized by. The yellow tip of a nuclear warhead peeked out from behind the clouds, lit by the early morning sun. It continued upward with what appeared to be… what was a soldier attached, his right arm wrapped around the missile, his left extended in flight. As the missile crested out of the clouds Artie saw another soldier carrying the rear of the missile as he flew! Soon there was a second missile carried by two more soldiers, then a third! As the final missile passed, Artie watched in shock as the seventh and final soldier summited the clouds. He was older, with a face carved from granite, and as he passed the F-16's, he smiled and saluted.

In an instant they disappeared into the atmosphere, into a dream. Artie squeezed the throttle, desperate to touch something real to ensure he was still part of this world and not whatever plane of reality on which those men existed.

"Promise me something, Fox Trot," he mumbled.
"Roger that, Yankee Delta."
He shook his head and looked to Hillman.
"If no one asks..."
"Yes?"
"We don't tell."

*

Newman smiled as he sailed through the clouds, the missile resting comfortably on his shoulder, the wind whipping him, ripping off layers of dirt and sweat and the brittle, dead scales that had covered him like armor for decades.

Back in the hangar he could not get airborne at first. He watched the other men give themselves over to the impossible feat and sail into the air, and flit around with Butterman, who turned out not to be such dead weight after all. They had flung themselves with such abandon, such fearlessness that they actually made it look easy. Newman had no choice but to follow, so he opened his chest to the sky, flung his arms back and closed his eyes, but nothing happened. He did it again, and again, nothing. He simply did not believe he could fly.

The jets roared ever closer and finally, on this third attempt, Newman stepped outside himself one final time to allow the old man to act without the reflexive pathology of his withered soul. Newman felt the old man forgive himself for the doubt and the shame, for all of his trespasses and failings. He felt the old man give thanks and felt his heart fill with hope, and love for himself and the unlikely platoon of six courageous men that fortune had surrounded him with. Newman stepped back inside the old man, and vowed never to leave again.

Instantly he was in the air. He thought for a passing moment of his father, his grandfather, the commanders and good men he had known, wondered what they would say if they knew, but such thoughts were anchors and as he flew, he let the wind rip them away and carry them off to die in the desert below. With the memories of his heroes discarded, Newman was left to think only of God. As the platoon ascended toward Him, Newman could not help but wonder if they were being observed at this very moment, defying Him in every way. However, for the first time in his life, he did not care what the answer was. If I can fly on my own, he thought, what do I need God for?

Chapter 24

Cadbury cut a blistering pace across the West Lawn. The corps had already begun the Washington Post March, his cue to take the stage. It was an exquisite spring day in Washington, D.C. and the cherry blossoms were in bloom, which meant tourists, and tourists meant traffic, and traffic in Washington D.C. was bad enough to run a good man out of town without the god forsaken cherry blossoms, but throw in a little arboreal splendor and the capital of the world grew tight as a nun's tush, as his mother used to say. He briefly considered begging the president's forgiveness with this same line of explanation, but thought better of it. The leader of the free world should have much bigger concerns now that his armed forces had turned seven of the good lord's perfect creations- originally made in His vision- into abominable sodomites. There would quite literally be hell to pay. Ever since those boys had flown themselves into United States airspace with Iraq's nuclear arsenal strapped to their backs some three days ago Cadbury had been waiting to be struck down like a dog. God's vengeance had not been visited upon him yet, but he was certain it was en route. He had not slept a wink in those 72 hours, only rocked in his smoking chair, the one by the front window, with a 12-gauge shotgun across his lap, a pistol strapped to his ankle, and the shih tzu, Agatha by his side. The Shih Tzu was his wife's but it was a light sleeper and insisted on watching him watch the front lawn for signs of the rapture, or at least the grim reaper, and if he was being honest, he thought, he enjoyed the company. If he could get the president's ear for just a few minutes he would be certain to mention all of this to him, if not for therapeutic reasons, at least to warn the man of the fire and brimstone headed his way. It would be the responsible thing to do, wouldn't it? No, he thought, that would signal doubt in his own ability to protect the country, and irreversibly diminish his standing with the president. He must not know of any of this, not a word. The handful of men involved in the bungling of the platoon's disappearance had already been dispatched with, and the only remaining insiders were on the stage at the end of the west lawn. He wouldn't dare send them on another suicide mission, lest they survive and bring back an entire army this time. He would have to bear this cross in silence like Jesus Christ himself. Perhaps that's why he was spared the wrath of God, he thought: he had already received his punishment directly from the almighty himself.

These ethereal fantasies were a brief flash of the madness that was to overtake him. Only a few months later Cadbury was caught naked and alone in the White House Situation Room, begging the commander of a submarine stationed in the Pacific Northwest to bomb positions in the Yukon Territory where he claimed to have proprietary knowledge of three nuclear weapons being hidden as a personal favor to him by the Canadian government. He was weeping openly and when confronted he attempted to strangle himself with the cord of the telephone. The expandable plastic cord barely left a mark. Secret Service was sufficiently spooked to revoke his clearances and he was replaced post-haste by the soft-spoken, well-liked General Howell during a polite and well-publicized ceremony. Cadbury would be awarded the Presidential Medal of Freedom for his service and retired to a compound in New Mexico. Howell would later instigate a third world war by claiming that Iraq had a small cache of nuclear weapons hidden in its northern mountains near the Turkish border, though he knew they were safely stowed 6,500 miles away, under the Canadian Rockies, miles below Tweedsmuir Provincial Park and Nature Reserve. He, too, would be awarded for his service.

Cadbury climbed onto the stage and took his seat next to the president and first lady. When he saw the platoon, a chill ran through him. They were even taller than he remembered, and their chests had broadened. He had always revered the strapping, thin diamond look of a well-drilled soldier- the smooth head atop wide shoulders and thick arms, the onlooker's line of vision drawn down past a narrowing waistline to a fine point at the shined shoes. These boys on stage were ten carats if they were one, he thought, depressed. Quickly his sadness turned to rage at the arrogance, the gall of these men to fly like that, to just take to the air without permission. Men were court martialed for less, good men in fact, not like these… And where was the apology? The army had to scramble two stealth fighters when these boys re-entered U.S. airspace, who's going to pay for that? And look at them now, shining, oblivious. They're oblivious to my pain, he thought. I have spent a lifetime protecting this nation, this Chosen nation, and my reward is the mockery of these… To add insult to injury I now have to pin the Medal of Honor on the chests of my tormenters, he lamented. Where's my medal? Where's the medal for my pain?

There would be no medal for Cadbury's pain, no balm, no remuneration. He would take this humiliation with him to the grave, what should have been a footnote becoming the very story of his life, and his undoing.

Newman glanced at the wild-eyed defense secretary who seemed to be glaring through his very soul. Just a few short weeks ago he would have followed this man into hell if commanded. Funny, he thought, how everything can change even when nothing changes. He was still General Newman Ginger, divorced engineer and estranged father. That cruel little man across the dais was still the leader of the greatest army the world had ever known, a man with the power to write history. But, somehow Newman's idolatry had evaporated in the fog of battle. The secretary seemed small now, silly. Perhaps it was because Newman would shortly become a highly decorated, honorably discharged civilian, perhaps it was because of the lingering effects of the gas, or the crowd, or the sunshine, but all he could see of the man was his age. He was a relic, shrinking and ossifying before Newman's eyes.

The president spoke broadly and kindly, either unaware of- or hiding- the specifics of the mission. Perhaps his handlers and message-shapers in all their wisdom had decided the nation was not ready for the story of the flying fags who carried nuclear weapons across the Pacific Ocean, saving themselves and quite possibly the world from nuclear annihilation. Or, perhaps nobody told him. How would that conversation go, Newman wondered? Where would one even start? He envisioned the decaying secretary requesting five minutes with the president, shuffling in with his tail between his legs, unshaven, unsteady, overwhelmed for the first time by the enormity of the office in which he was standing.

The horror of the imagined moment lingered after the scene itself had disappeared. Newman was suddenly awash with shame- it had not been long ago that he, too was horrified by the men standing next to him. The distance between him and Cadbury may be miles now, but it was once inches.

He embraced the shame, followed the thread of it inward and around and down to its root and what he saw at the very beginning was not the platoon or the secretary, it was not homosexuality, it was the girls. The arms-length distance at which he kept them had grown to a gulf before they were old enough to drive, and as soon as they could motor away to seemingly infinite distances, they did. Soon, calls went unreturned, letters went unanswered and a father became a polite but silent fixture at holidays, like the Christmas tree, or, he often thought, the blood red candles the girls placed next to the centerpiece, that grew smaller and smaller each year. He resolved to visit each of them- via a traditional airliner, in accordance with his settlement with the Department of Defense- and embark on the next great mission of his life: reconciliation.

He looked down the line at his beaming boys. Only one would stay and serve, Richards. The rest would go on, first, to make sense of themselves and then to find fulfilling careers, or at least steady paychecks. None of the men would fly again, in fact, as all were loyal law-abiding servicemen who agreed to nondisclosure and permanent grounding in return for an honorable discharge and a modest severance.

Cadbury was certainly grateful for their cooperation, as it ensured there were no loose ends. He would never learn of the small vile of O.C.D., hidden in a porcelain figurine of the Blessed Virgin Mary that Newman discovered tucked deep in his pack. It was a gift- more likely an insurance policy- from the scientist. Newman had forgotten to use the elixir back on the mountain, and it had somehow survived the long flight west. Now it was his, and his alone. He squeezed it gently in his pocket, thanked God, and closed his eyes.

Cadbury harumphed into his seat next to the president after pinning the Medal of Honor onto each of the boys- a rather humiliating experience, as each wore the same shit-grin and, he wasn't positive, but he could've sworn the black one winked at him.

"Is it just me," whispered the president, "or is there something funny about these boys?"

Cadbury studied his face for a brief second and saw the president was clueless.

"Don't ask."

Love Bomb and the Pink Platoon

Ryan Gielen

Published by BROWNPENNY

ISBN 978-0-9850493-1-7

For updates on the book, AudioBook, author and film, please visit **www.lovebombbook.com**.

Please take a second to "Like" the book on Facebook!

Finally, please write a review on Amazon, or iTunes, or both. Your thoughtful reviews are paramount to the success of the book!

Thank you for reading *Love Bomb and the Pink Platoon.*

- Ryan

P.S. the book trailer will be available on YouTube and Vimeo on February 14th. Google it and share it, if you're so inclined.

Made in the USA
Lexington, KY
18 December 2013